Acting Edition

Dial M
For Murder

Adapted by Jeffrey Hatcher

From the original by
Frederick Knott

FOR PRODUCTION INQUIRIES

UNITED STATES AND CANADA
info@concordtheatricals.com
1-866-979-0447

UNITED KINGDOM AND EUROPE
licensing@concordtheatricals.co.uk
020-7054-7298

Each title is subject to availability from Concord Theatricals Corp.,
depending upon country of performance. Please be aware that *DIAL
M FOR MURDER* may not be licensed by Concord Theatricals Corp. in
your territory. Professional and amateur producers should contact the
nearest Concord Theatricals Corp. office or licensing partner to verify
availability.

This work is published by Samuel French, an imprint of Concord
Theatricals Corp.

DIAL M FOR MURDER received its world premiere on July 28, 2022 at The Old Globe, San Diego. Artistic Director, Barry Edelstein; Managing Director, Timothy J. Shields. Directed by Stafford Arima. The cast was as follows:

MARGOT WENDICE . . . . .Kate Abbruzzese

MAXINE HADLEY . . . . Ruibo Qian

TONY WENDICE . . . . Nathan Darrow

LESGATE . . . . Ruy Iskandar

INSPECTOR HUBBARD . . . . John Tufts

CHARACTERS

MARGOT WENDICE – 30s/40s, English
MAXINE HADLEY – 30s/40s, American
TONY WENDICE – 30s/40s, English
LESGATE – 30s/40s, English)
INSPECTOR HUBBARD – 40s/50s, English

SETTING

The living room of the Wendice flat in London, 1952.

TIME

ACT ONE

Scene One – A Friday evening in September.
Scene Two – Saturday evening.
Scene Three – Later that night.

ACT TWO

Scene One – The next morning.
Scene Two – A few months later. Afternoon.

AUTHOR'S NOTE

Set Design

When Old Globe artistic director Barry Edelstein asked me to adapt Frederick Knott's wonderful play *Dial M For Murder*, he said the production would be in their Sheryl and Harvey White in-the-round theater. At first I thought this would be a challenge, given that "Dial M" is classically a proscenium show. But between Stafford Arima's brilliant direction and Anna Louizos' terrific stage design, we were able to create a space that worked beautifully, even though we had no doors, and the off-stage bedroom was accessed via a flight of steps that went through the audience. For this published version, the stage directions reflect the original's proscenium setting, but with minor adjustments it works just as well for in-the-round or thrust.

Sound

In Act One, Scene Three, we hear the BBC interview that Margot is listening to. The parts of the interview that should be heard clearly by the audience are in the script, but the audience should be aware of the interview at a lower level throughout the scene. So you will need to record a longer version of the interview, edit it to match your stage action and adjust the volume at the right moments. A longer version of the BBC interview transcript is available at the back of the script.

ACT ONE

Scene One

(Living Room.)

(The Wendice flat.)

(The sitting room of a ground floor flat in a large house which has been converted into apartments.)

(Upstage right are French doors that look out onto a garden.)

(Upstage left is a door to the bedroom. Next to it a door to the kitchen.)

(Upstage center is the front door that leads to the ground floor hall. The door has a Yale-type lock. When this door is open, we can see into the hall which leads to the street door. Back of this hall is a staircase leading up [from stage left to stage right] to the flat above. The stairs pass the front door at about the fifth step.)

(The flat is expensively furnished. Sofa, chairs, coffee table, window seat, drinks table, a desk and chair in front of the French doors. On the desk is a telephone. On the coffee table is a silver cigarette box.)

(There is a coat rack near the front door.)

(Next to the drinks table is a wastebasket.)

(Next to the sofa is a mending basket.)

(It's seven-thirty p.m. Friday evening. September.)

(MARGOT *and* **MAXINE** *are drinking cocktails.* **MAXINE** *smokes.)*

MARGOT. So. How would you murder me?

MAXINE. How would you *like* to be murdered?

MARGOT. What are my choices?

MAXINE. Oh, there are so many methods to choose from. Alphabetically there's asphyxiation, blade, bludgeon, bullet...

MARGOT. Blow to the head?

MAXINE. Same as bludgeon really.

MARGOT. Sorry.

MAXINE. Drowning. Electrocution. Garroting. Hanging. Poison. Strangling.

MARGOT. Isn't strangling the same as garroting?

MAXINE. Garroting is a subcategory of strangling.

MARGOT. I see.

MAXINE. Truth be told, they're both subcategories of asphyxiation.

MARGOT. God is in the details. Go on.

MAXINE. Shoot. Stab. Erm...

MARGOT. You're up to T.

MAXINE. Tickle to death?

MARGOT. It's been tried.

MAXINE. Yes, I know, you're immune.

MARGOT. *(Beat.)* You're disturbingly good at this.

MAXINE. It's all I've thought about for the past year.

MARGOT. Murder?

MAXINE. Means, motives, killer and killed.

MARGOT. It would defeat me. Having to come up with the motive alone. I mean, how many motives are there, really?

MAXINE. Five.

MARGOT. Five?

MAXINE. Five for murder, yes.

MARGOT. I'll bet I can guess them.

MAXINE. Go on.

MARGOT. Money. Fear. Jealousy. Revenge... Uhm... five you said?

MAXINE. I did, yes.

MARGOT. I give up.

MAXINE. Protecting someone you love. *(Beat.)* Was it all right, my dropping by? I mean, we *had* said we'd meet at the theater, the three of us.

MARGOT. No, this is better, seeing you without Tony.

MAXINE. Why?

MARGOT. There's something I wanted to tell you. When Tony let me know you were coming to London about your book, I knew I couldn't put it off any longer.

MAXINE. Better top this off then.

(**MARGOT** *refreshes their drinks.*)

MARGOT. After you went back to New York last year and wrote to me, I...I burned all your letters. All except one. You probably know the one I mean.

MAXINE. I think I can guess.

MARGOT. I carried it wherever I went. Then one weekend Tony and I were going away. We were at Victoria Station. The letter was in my handbag. But that day, I set my bag down to pay for something and when I turned back it was gone.

MAXINE. Did you get it back?

MARGOT. *(Nods.)* We reported it, and a week later the bag showed up in the lost and found. But the letter wasn't in it. A few days later I got this.

(**MARGOT** *gives* **MAXINE** *a small note.*)

MAXINE. *(Reads.)* "Am in possession of a letter belonging to you. If you wish its return, place five thousand pounds in a package and leave it for John S. King, 23 Newport Street, SW7." Done in block capital letters. Anyone could have written this. What did you do?

MARGOT. Nothing.

MAXINE. Didn't you want it back? Five thousand pounds couldn't have made much of a difference to *you.*

MARGOT. Of course I wanted it back. But I was terrified to make a move. Then I received a second note.

(**MARGOT** *gives* **MAXINE** *a second note.*)

MAXINE. *(Reads.)* "If you do not deliver five thousand pounds to John S. King at 23 Newport Street by this Friday, the letter will be given to your husband."

MARGOT. So I took five thousand pounds out of the bank, put it in a parcel and left it at 23 Newport Street. It's a little shop people use as a forwarding address.

MAXINE. And then?

MARGOT. Then I waited for the letter to be returned, but...nothing came. After a week, I went back. They said a messenger had picked up the parcel.

MAXINE. You never heard from the blackmailer again?

MARGOT. No.

MAXINE. Is that why you told me to stop writing?

MARGOT. *(Nods.)* I imagined any letter you wrote to me being stolen and read.

MAXINE. *(Re: notes.)* May I hold on to these for a while?

MARGOT. *(Shrugs.)* If you like.

(**MAXINE** *puts the notes into her purse.*)

MAXINE. You never told Tony?

MARGOT. No, and I never will.

(Beat.)

That night I went to your flat to say good-bye, Tony was driving to Oxford for the weekend. When I came back here, I collapsed onto that sofa and cried for hours. Eventually I fell asleep. Then I woke, and Tony was standing there, looking down on me. He said he'd got halfway to Oxford when suddenly he knew that he had to give up writing and take that job at your publishers.

MAXINE. Yes, he called me next morning and said the same thing. Public relations. I hear he's very good at it.

MARGOT. It's his great talent, charming people.

MAXINE. Did he say why he was giving up on his writing?

MARGOT. He said he wanted to become the husband I deserved.

MAXINE. And has he been?

MARGOT. I think he believes he's tried.

MAXINE. And that's good enough for you?

> (**MARGOT** *looks at* **MAXINE**. **MAXINE** *returns her stare. A thousand emotions pass between them: affection, regret, resentment.*)
>
> (**MAXINE** *opens the cigarette box, takes out a cigarette, lights it, and smokes.*)

That night. A year ago. I'm standing there in that closet called a flat, slicing button mushrooms for the spaghetti, thinking: "I'm going to make Margot tell Tony everything, have it out with him."

MARGOT. You know it never could have worked.

MAXINE. It?

MARGOT. We. Us.

MAXINE. Because?

MARGOT. Because it couldn't! It...!

> (*Beat.*)

I've told you about my aunt.

MAXINE. Your aunt who never married and left you everything.

MARGOT. She knew me very well. When Tony proposed and I was on the fence about saying "yes," she was quite clear about what I should do.

MAXINE. Did she think marriage would make you happy?

MARGOT. Happier than *she'd* been.

MAXINE. So to please your rich, unmarried, unhappy aunt who was, in every way but her predilections, boringly conventional and afraid of scandal, you married Tony, the consequence of which is that you are as unhappy as she was, only for different reasons. At least you got her money when she died. (**MARGOT** *is stunned.* **MAXINE** *changes gears.*) Why didn't you tell me about these blackmail notes when you got them?

MARGOT. I don't know. I was confused. And I...I thought it might have been you.

MAXINE. You thought I sent you these blackmail notes?

MARGOT. You were so angry with me, flying back to New York like that!

MAXINE. Yes, flying to New York, writing you letters every day, until you told me to stop. I couldn't stay here in London knowing you were trying to make a go of it with Tony. Do you know how I spent the past year? I got the cheapest apartment I could find, a sixth floor walk-up in Greenwich Village, and I typed. Rather I smoked and typed. Rather I smoked and drank a half bottle of whiskey a day and typed, but the whiskey was only at the end of the day, it was the reward for my work. If I wrote a thousand words, I could have a drink.

I thought, if I don't finish this book, what was it all for, all the mess and roiling passions? So I smoked and I typed and I finished it. That's how I spent the last year since you broke things off. That's how I filled my days.

(*A light cocktail chat voice.*)

And how do you fill *yours*?

MARGOT. I keep house, I volunteer. At the museum.

MAXINE. Which? London has so many.

MARGOT. The British Museum and the National and the Tate and the Portrait Gallery. I'm part of a group that goes into the East End to see to women who don't have it as good as... I'm mad for the theater, evenings and matinees, you'll always find me there, sixth row center.

I've taken up Indonesian cooking. I gave up smoking. And there's Tony.

MAXINE. And does that fill your days?

MARGOT. Not one bit.

> *(Sound of a key in the front door.)*

> (**MARGOT** *and* **MAXINE** *turn away from each other as –)*

> (**TONY** *enters. He wears a raincoat and carries a briefcase.)*

MAXINE. There's the boy!

MARGOT. Tony, where have you been?

TONY. Sorry, darlings, an emergency blew up just as I was trying to leave.

> (**TONY** *kisses* **MARGOT.***)*

MAXINE. Aren't you going to kiss *me*?

TONY. I was observing the formalities: first the wife, *then* the lover.

MAXINE. You and I were never lovers.

TONY. Quite right, a dozen dinner dates does not a lover make.

> (**TONY** *kisses* **MAXINE.** *Then he goes to the drinks table and pours a drink.)*

So, what have you two been conspiring about? "Plots have I laid, inductions dangerous"?

MARGOT. Don't fix yourself a drink, you've no time. The play starts in less than –

TONY. Yes, I know, and...I can't go.

MARGOT. What?

MAXINE. But the play's a murder mystery, and it's supposed to be dreadful, we'll have such a good time.

TONY. I know, and I'm sorry, but I've got to revise the jacket copy for your book.

MAXINE. I thought that had been done months ago.

TONY. It was, but the boss says it needs to be completely re-done. It's got to be ready first thing tomorrow, so I've no choice.

MAXINE. Can't you dash off something in the morning?

TONY. In the morning, you and I have breakfast with the editor of the *Times Sunday Supplement*, then a meeting about the cover art. I told them you hate the colors, lurid you called them.

MAXINE. Not lurid *enough*.

TONY. They're showing you some new ideas based on the same look.

MAXINE. Woman, corpse, blood?

TONY. It's what sells.

MARGOT. Lovely.

MAXINE. When's the BBC interview?

TONY. Tomorrow evening at eight o'clock. Very good time slot. You'll be listened to by every wife, widow and pensioner in the country.

MAXINE. My readership.

TONY. And we're having supper after.

MARGOT. *(To **MAXINE**.)* Where would you like to go?

MAXINE. *(To **MARGOT**.)* Where would *you* like to go?

TONY. *(To **MARGOT**.)* Uhm, darling? Pottifer is joining us for dinner tomorrow night.

MARGOT. Oh, Lord.

MAXINE. Who's Pottifer?

TONY. The BBC talks director. Dinner with him is the price of that awfully good time slot.

(*To* **MARGOT.**) I know you loathe him, so I explained you were otherwise engaged.

MARGOT. Ah. Well. Thanks for getting me off the hook. I will now spend a lonely evening at home.

(*To* **MAXINE.**) So I won't see you at all tomorrow?

TONY. The studios are just across the park. We'll all have a drink here before we go. That all right, Maxine?

MAXINE. Sure, I'm easy.

TONY. (*Checks his watch.*) Oh. I'd better call and get you a taxi.

MARGOT. Don't bother. We can pick one up at the corner.

TONY. All right, but you'd better go now then.

MAXINE. Come on, let's make a run for it.

> (**MAXINE** *and* **MARGOT** *finish their drinks, pick up their purses and gloves, and open the front door.*)

MARGOT. What do you want us to do with your ticket, try to give it away?

TONY. Sell it, have a drink on the proceeds.

MAXINE. Should be good for two drinks. Margot. Your handbag.

> (**MARGOT** *picks up her forgotten handbag.*)

> (*A final flurry of* "Goodnights" *as* **MAXINE** *and* **MARGOT** *exit.*)

(**TONY** *closes the door.*)

(*He surveys the living room for a moment. Checks his watch. Finishes his drink. Then goes into gear.*)

(*He takes the three cocktail glasses and sets them on the drinks table.*)

(*He dumps the ashes from the ashtray into the wastebasket.*)

(*He sets the ashtray back on the coffee table.*)

(*He opens the briefcase, takes out a framed photograph, and places it on the desk as if that's where it always sits.*)

(*He takes a pair of white cotton gloves from his raincoat pocket and puts them on the arm of the sofa.*)

(*We hear the front door buzzer.*)

(**TONY** *checks his watch again.*)

(*He kneels next to the sofa, feels under it, and retrieves a cane. He stands and, assuming a painful limp, uses the cane and opens the front door.*)

(**LESGATE** *stands there, sports jacket, rakish moustache.*)

LESGATE. Mr. Fisher?

TONY. Stephen Fisher, yes. Captain Lesgate?

LESGATE. Yes.

TONY. Do come in.

(**LESGATE** *enters.*)

(**TONY** *closes the front door.*)

LESGATE. I'm a tad early. Hope you don't mind.

TONY. No, no, not at all, keep me on my toes. Did you have any difficulty finding your way?

LESGATE. None at all.

TONY. Drink?

LESGATE. Love one.

> (**LESGATE** *watches* **TONY** *limp to the drinks table.*)

By the way, how did you know my car was for sale?

TONY. Your garage told me. I stopped for a fill-up and saw it on the blocks. I said I was looking for something like it, and they gave me your phone number. It *is* still for sale, I hope.

LESGATE. If you've got eleven hundred pounds.

TONY. I refuse to discuss the price until you've had at least three brandies.

> (**TONY** *hands* **LESGATE** *his glass.*)

LESGATE. I warn you, I drive a hard bargain, drunk or sober.

> (*They drink.*)

> (**LESGATE** *sits on the sofa.*)

> (**TONY** *sits opposite him.*)

I can't help thinking I've seen you before somewhere.

TONY. Funny you should say that. The moment I opened the door, I... wait a minute. Lesgate? No. Not Lesgate. Swann! C.J. Swann. Or was it C.A.?

LESGATE. *(Wary now.)* ...C.A.

TONY. You were at Cambridge. Must be twenty years ago. You wouldn't remember me. I think you only came my last year.

LESGATE. Yes, of course. But I don't recall anyone named Fisher.

TONY. That's because my name's not Fisher. It's Wendice.

LESGATE. That's right, Tony Wendice. So what's all this about "Fisher"?

TONY. *(Smiles.)* What's all this about "Lesgate"?

LESGATE. I got bored. Thought it was time for a trade up. Don't you like it?

TONY. *Love* it.

> *(They drink, smiling at each other over their glasses.)*
>
> *(Beat.)*

Would you like a cigar?

LESGATE. I'll stick to my pipe, if you don't mind.

TONY. That's one habit you've changed. At college you used to smoke rather expensive cigars. Here, look at this.

> *(**TONY** stands and limps to the desk. He picks up the framed photograph and brings it over to **LESGATE**.)*

A photo of us all at a reunion dinner. There you are, chewing on a huge Havana.

LESGATE. That must be ten years ago. The first and last reunion I ever went to. What a murderous thug I look.

TONY. You do rather. Of course, I always remember you because of the College Ball. You were treasurer the year the ticket money was stolen, weren't you?

LESGATE. Nearly a hundred pounds. I'd left it in a cash box in my study. In the morning, it had gone.

TONY. It was the college porter, of course.

LESGATE. Yes, poor old Alfred. They found the cash box in his back garden.

TONY. But not the money.

LESGATE. No.

> (**LESGATE** *hands the photo to* **TONY** *who limps back to put it on the desk.*)

TONY. What are you doing nowadays?

LESGATE. A little of this, a little of that. What about you?

TONY. I work for a publishing house.

LESGATE. Books, eh? Must do well by it. You have a very comfortable set-up.

TONY. My wife has money.

LESGATE. Ah. People with capital don't realize how lucky they are. I'm resigned to living on what I can earn.

TONY. You could marry for money.

LESGATE. Yes, I suppose some people make a profession of that.

TONY. I know *I* did.

LESGATE. You mean the girl you fell in love with happened to have some money of her own?

TONY. No, I married for money, quite deliberately.

LESGATE. Well – that's putting it bluntly.

TONY. Have I shocked you?

LESGATE. No, I always admire a man who knows what he wants.

TONY. To know what you want to *pay* for, that's the thing. Everything has its price.

LESGATE. Yes, quite. (*Looking at his wrist watch.*) I haven't a great deal of time –

TONY. I was telling you about marrying my wife.

LESGATE. Yes, your "profession."

TONY. Oh, I had a profession before that. A vocation really. I was a writer.

LESGATE. Would I have read anything you've written?

TONY. Not unless you had a job rejecting manuscripts.

LESGATE. I see. So you gave it up. Before or after you married for money?

TONY. Oh, after. My wife was very taken with the idea of being married to a writer. There's something about a tortured novelist burning with things to say and looking damn good while he's not saying them. Full of promise which didn't pan out.

LESGATE. She hasn't left you because of it.

TONY. She nearly did. Oh, not because I gave up on the writing. Get you another?

> (**TONY** *stands to refresh their drinks, winces painfully.*)

LESGATE. Let me. You've got that groggy leg.

TONY. Thanks. Move the bottle over here. Would you like to hear about it? How my wife nearly left me.

LESGATE. Your party, your brandy.

TONY. It is, yes. I used to go around with a woman, another writer, more successful than me, by which I mean she was successful. In those days, she'd written only short stories. Thrillers. Naturally, I pretended to look down on her stuff. I was a "serious" writer. About the same time, I met this other girl, very pretty, with a nice inheritance in the offing. We got married and set up here. Very placid and pleasant. I wrote like a demon, but I couldn't get any what-the-Americans-call *action*. Lots of *activity* though. I was always going off to do readings of this or that unpublished novel. Oxford. Cambridge. If it were a slow season, I'd go to Edinburgh. Lord, I went to Wales once. There were always people in the audience to listen to me. Women mostly. Young. My wife professed not to like that.

LESGATE. With or without reason?

TONY. With very good reason. You see, long after I'd realized that I wasn't getting action, I still enjoyed the activity: the travel, the stipend, the adoring faces, the charming room at the college inn or the department chair's guest cottage. I thought I was being clever, pulling the wool over my wife's eyes. I figured she wouldn't catch on. But you know what happened?

LESGATE. She caught on?

TONY. No. *I* did.

LESGATE. To what?

TONY. She was having an affair. The usual tells: she lost weight, there were phone calls that would end abruptly when I came into the room. Then we had a row. I wanted to go to Oxford for the weekend, she didn't want me to. I went into the bedroom to pack. Then the phone rang in here. It all sounded pretty urgent. After she rang off, she suddenly was rather keen that I should go to Oxford after all. So I packed my kit into the car, drove off, parked two streets away and came back.

Five minutes later she came out and took a taxi. I followed. She got out in Bywater Street, an address I knew well. I looked in through a window, and what do you think I saw?

LESGATE. I've no idea.

TONY. My wife. In the arms of a woman.

LESGATE. Ohhh.

TONY. Can you guess who the other woman was?

LESGATE. *(Thinks, then.)* The female writer of thrillers?

TONY. Well done!

LESGATE. Bit of a coincidence, that, don't you think?

TONY. By no means. I had introduced them. My friend, my wife. And me blissfully unawares, going off on my little jaunts to play with young poetesses and disappointed faculty wives.

LESGATE. I can't imagine how you must have felt.

TONY. Try.

LESGATE. I'd be in a bloody rage. I'd feel like giving them both a good bashing.

TONY. Ah, now, I suspected you and I would be similar in that respect. We don't like women enjoying the upper hand, do we?

LESGATE. Did you burst in on them or –?

TONY. Lord, no. I watched. They were cooking spaghetti over a gas ring. Funny how you can tell when two people are in love. They were sharing a cigarette, just like in the movies.

The two of them seemed to be in the middle of a serious discussion. Then it became an argument, then tears, then my wife left. No one ate the spaghetti.

LESGATE. What did you do?

TONY. I went down to a pub at the end of the street and proceeded to drink heavily. I wondered: Was she going to leave me? What would happen if she *did* leave? There was no question of me leaving her. No, I'd grown to depend on her. All these expensive tastes I'd acquired. I sat there and thought of three different ways of killing the other woman. I thought of a few more of killing my wife. That seemed by far the more sensible route. Margot and I had just made our wills, leaving everything we had to each other. Hers worked out at just over two million pounds. When I returned home that night, there was Margot right where you're sitting, asleep, that pillow stained with tears. I looked down on her for a long time. Then her eyes opened and she looked up at me, and I told her my writing days were over. As fortune would have it, a publisher I knew had offered me a job. He was never going to publish my books, but he thought I could be useful in public relations. I threw myself into it, and in three months I was assistant head of publicity. In six, I'd taken over the top job. They can't do without me now. And irony: I'm in charge of the sales push for the other woman's first novel. She's just arrived in London to promote it.

LESGATE. She left England?

TONY. Turns out the spaghetti was a farewell dinner. They'd broken it off, that night. There were letters, though, after, from New York. They usually arrived on Thursdays. My wife burnt all of them except one. That one she would transfer from handbag to handbag, it was always with her. That letter became an obsession. I had to find out what was in it, so I stole it.

LESGATE. You stole your wife's love letter?

TONY. I even wrote her two anonymous notes offering to sell it back.

LESGATE. Why?

TONY. Malice. I was hoping it would make her come and confess everything, beg my forgiveness. But she didn't.

LESGATE. Christ. Did she pay up?

TONY. Five thousand pounds. But I kept the letter.

> (**TONY** *takes out his wallet and lets a letter fall out of it onto the floor.* **TONY** *starts to bend down, but he winces.*)

LESGATE. I'll get it.

> (**TONY** *watches as* **LESGATE** *picks up the letter.*)

TONY. Go on. Read.

> (*Gestures to the letter,* **LESGATE** *opens it, reads.*)

LESGATE. Very, erm, explicit.

TONY. Yes.

> (**LESGATE** *puts the letter back into Tony's wallet.* **TONY** *snaps it shut.*)

Anyway, they must have had the fear of God put into them because after that the letters stopped. Funny to think that just a year ago I was sitting in that pub, actually planning to murder my wife. And I might have done it if I hadn't seen something that changed my mind.

LESGATE. What was it you saw?

TONY. I saw you.

LESGATE. ...What was so odd about that?

TONY. The coincidence. Only a week before I'd been to a reunion dinner and the fellows had been talking about you, how you'd been court-martialed during the war, then a year in prison. That was news. Mind you, at college we'd always said Swann would end up in jail. That cash box. Everybody knew Alfred didn't take that money, you did.

LESGATE. *(Reddens, stands.)* Thanks for the drink. I take it you won't be wanting that car after all.

TONY. Don't you want me to tell you why I brought you here?

LESGATE. *(Beat.)* Yes, I think you'd better.

> *(During the next speech,* **TONY** *drops his limp, takes out his handkerchief, and wipes fingerprints off anything* **LESGATE** *touched.)*

TONY. As I say, it was quite a coincidence, seeing you in The Grape and Vine, just down the street from that flat. I asked about and found that you rented a room above the pub. You weren't Lesgate yet. The owner of The Grape and Vine knew you as "Pryce-Jones." I liked the hyphen. Would you mind passing me your glass? Thank you so much. You see, since that first night at the pub, I've been following you. I was hoping that, sooner or later, I might catch you at something, so I could, well, not to put too fine a point on it...

LESGATE. Blackmail me?

TONY. Influence you. After a few weeks, I got to know your routine which made it a lot easier.

LESGATE. Rather dull work.

TONY. It was, a bit, at first, but you know how it is, you take up a hobby and the more you get to know of it the more fascinating it becomes. You became *quite* fascinating. In fact, there were times when I felt that you belonged to me. You moved from The Grape and Vine and took lodgings in South Kensington under the name "Asprey." Six weeks later, you disappeared, owing six weeks rent and fifty pounds borrowed from your landlady.

(**LESGATE** *reaches for the brandy.*)

If you want another drink, do you mind putting on these gloves? Your new lodgings were in Belsize Park. There Mr. Asprey became Mr. Waterhouse. Mr. Waterhouse left *those* lodgings owing fifteen weeks rent and somewhat richer for his brief encounter with a Miss Wallace. Miss Wallace was in love with you, wasn't she? I suppose she thought you were growing that handsome mustache to please her. Poor Miss Wallace. By summer you'd moved to another flat owned by a Mrs. Van Dorn whose late husband left her two hotels and a very large apartment house. That's where you became Captain Lesgate. The only trouble is, Mrs. Van Dorn does rather enjoy being courted, and she is very expensive. Perhaps that's why you've been trying to sell her car for over a month.

LESGATE. Mrs. Van Dorn asked me to sell it for her.

TONY. I know. I called her up earlier today. She only wanted eight hundred.

(*Beat.*)

LESGATE. Where's the nearest police station?

TONY. Opposite the church, two minutes walk.

LESGATE. Suppose I go there now?

TONY. What would you tell them?

LESGATE. I shall tell them you're trying to blackmail me into...

TONY. Yes?

LESGATE. Murdering your wife.

TONY. And if you did, I'd say you came here tonight, half drunk, and tried to borrow money on the strength that we were at college together. When I refused you said something about a letter belonging to my wife. As far as I could make out you were offering to sell it to me. I gave you what money I had and you gave me the letter. It has your fingerprints on it. Remember?

Then you said if I went to the police you'd tell some crazy story about my wanting you to murder my wife. But before we go any further, consider the inconvenience. I'd have to tell the police Captain Lesgate's name is really Swann. The tricky thing there is that C.A. Swann died four years ago. Yes, I found the obituary. Motoring accident, body burned beyond recognition. I take it whomever you put behind the wheel was your first victim.

LESGATE. What do you mean, "first"?

TONY. Well, I mean to say, I *assume* he was the first, just as I assume the second was Miss Wallace. She was in all the papers. Middle-aged woman found dead from drug overdose. No one knows who gave the stuff to her. But we know, don't we? Poor Miss Wallace. And now you're planning to marry Mrs. Van Dorn, am I right?

LESGATE. Smart, aren't you?

TONY. Not really, I've just had time to think things out, put myself in your position. That's why I know you're going to agree.

LESGATE. Why?

TONY. For the same reason that a donkey with a stick behind him and a carrot in front goes forwards and not backwards.

LESGATE. Tell me about the carrot.

TONY. Five thousand pounds in cash.

LESGATE. For a murder?

TONY. For a few minutes work. At no risk. I do think a honeymoon with Mrs. Van Dorn would be preferable to the hangman's noose. Five thousand pounds should see you safely married and on the Continent. You'll find it makes such a difference to have money in your pocket.

LESGATE. This five thousand pounds, where is it?

> (**TONY** *opens the briefcase, shows its contents to* **LESGATE.**)

Is that the five thousand pounds she..?

TONY. Uh hm.

LESGATE. How much is there?

TONY. The full amount. I don't think you'll do a runner, not with Mrs. Van Dorn in your future and me knowing about Miss Wallace and the rest.

LESGATE. When would this take place?

TONY. Tomorrow night.

LESGATE. Tomorrow?! Not a chance.

TONY. It's got to be tomorrow, I've arranged things that way.

LESGATE. Where?

TONY. Approximately where you're standing now.

LESGATE. How?

TONY. Tomorrow evening, at exactly eight o'clock you will enter the house by the street door. The street door is always unlocked.

> (**TONY** *opens the front door, steps into the hall and points to the fifth step of the staircase.*)

You'll find the key to the front door under the stair carpet out in the hall. On the fifth step.

LESGATE. The fifth step.

TONY. That's the one. Use it to unlock the front door...

> *(Re-enters, closes front door, moves to French doors.)*

...and go straight to hide in the alcove.

LESGATE. What if she's right here?

TONY. She won't be. She'll be listening to a radio program. The radio is in our bedroom. At exactly ten minutes past eight that phone will ring. It will be me, telephoning from the BBC studios across Regents Park. That's my alibi. The radio program's an interview with the female novelist. I shall be there with her.

LESGATE. All right, then.

TONY. I shall use the phone in the control booth. I shall dial this number. There's no extension in the bedroom, so when the phone rings she will come in here to answer it. You stay hidden in that alcove until she answers the phone. When you've finished, pick up the phone and give me a soft whistle. Then hang up. When I hear your whistle I shall hang up.

LESGATE. What happens then?

TONY. Make a mess of things. Upend the coffee table, knock over that cigarette box and those silver trays. But leave it all here.

LESGATE. As if I left in a hurry?

TONY. *(Nods.)* Now the French doors. If they're locked, unlock them and leave them open. Then go out exactly the same way as you came in.

LESGATE. By the front door?

TONY. Yes. And here's the most important thing. As you go out, return the key to the place where you found it.

LESGATE. Under the fifth stair carpet?

TONY. The police will assume you entered by way of the French doors. You thought the flat was empty and went to work. She heard something and came in here. You attacked her. When you realized you'd killed her, you panicked and bolted into the garden leaving your loot behind.

LESGATE. Just a minute. I'm *supposed* to have entered through the French doors. What if they're locked?

TONY. She often takes a walk round the garden before she goes to bed and she usually forgets to lock those doors when she gets back. That's what I'll tell the police.

LESGATE. But she may say...

TONY. But she isn't going to say anything. Is she?

LESGATE. Why can't I just leave by way of the garden?

TONY. There's an iron gate to the street. It's locked at night, so you'd have to climb over it. If anyone saw you, you'd likely be followed.

LESGATE. Right. So, I leave the flat, put the key back under the stair carpet, and go out by the street door. When will you get back?

TONY. About eleven. I'll bring the other woman back here for a nightcap. We shall find her together.

LESGATE. You've forgotten something. When you return, how will you get into the flat?

TONY. I'll let myself in.

LESGATE. But your key will be under the stair carpet. The other woman is bound to see you take it out. It'll give the whole show away.

TONY. No, it won't be my key under the carpet. It will be my wife's. I'll take it from her handbag and hide it out there just before I leave the flat. She won't be going out tomorrow night so she won't miss it. When I return I'll use my own key to let us in. Then, before the police arrive, I'll find a moment to take her key from under the stair carpet and return it to her handbag.

LESGATE. How many keys are there to that door?

TONY. Two keys. Just hers and mine.

> *(Telephone rings.)*

> *(**TONY** goes to the desk and picks up phone.)*

> *(As **TONY** speaks, **LESGATE** picks up the cotton gloves and puts them on.)*

Maida Vale 0401. – Hullo, darling, how's it going? – Dreadful? – Good. Does Maxine hate it as much as you? – Make a bet on who the killer is, and tell me who wins.

> *(**TONY** sees **LESGATE** start to the French doors.)*

Oh, darling, just a minute, I think there's someone at the door. *(To **LESGATE**, muffling telephone.)* Careful, you might be seen from there. *(Into phone.)* Sorry, darling, false alarm. No, go, go. – Enjoy yourself.

> *(**TONY** hangs up.)*

Well?

> *(**LESGATE** pauses, undecided. Then he looks inside the open briefcase.)*

> *(**LESGATE** snaps the briefcase shut, and picks it up.)*

> *(**TONY** smiles.)*

End of Scene One

Scene Two

(The same.)

(Saturday evening.)

(Seven-twenty p.m.)

(Maxine's fur is hung on the coat rack next to Tony's raincoat.)

(Margot's handbag is set on the table behind the sofa.)

(Margot sits in a chair, dressed in a sweater and slacks.)

(Maxine, dressed to go out, sits on the sofa. She smokes.)

(They both have cocktails.)

MARGOT. Do you enjoy thinking up ways to kill people?

MAXINE. I never have to *think* up ways of killing people. Ways of killing people bubble up in my head all the time. I'm simply putting my natural instincts to good use.

> *(Now we see that* **MARGOT** *is reading questions from a typed sheet.)*

MARGOT. *(Reads.)* "Can anyone be a killer"?

MAXINE. Oh, yes. Given the right circumstances. Any of us, even the nicest, most passive milquetoast can be a killer.

> *(****TONY**** enters from the bedroom in a tuxedo. He goes to the drinks table to mix a drink.)*

Note that I did not say murderer. Murder is a legal term. One can kill with moral intent. That's what we call it in war.

TONY. I'm not sure you need to get into all that.

MAXINE. Well, it's true.

MARGOT. She's right, it is.

TONY. I know, but it's a talks program about thrillers, not moral philosophy. They've got Bertrand Russell for that. Read that last question, would you, darling?

MARGOT. *(Reads.)* "Is there such a thing as a perfect murder? And if so, can you cite an example"?

MAXINE. If I could cite an example, it wouldn't be a perfect murder. There are people who've committed murders who walk amongst us every day, on the street, in tea shops, at the pub. A murderer might be sitting on your sofa or lying next to you in bed.

MARGOT. That's very good.

MAXINE. Thank you.

TONY. Right, that's the lot.

> (**TONY** *takes the sheet of questions from* **MARGOT**.)

MARGOT. Won't they ask what you're working on next? They always do on programs like these.

TONY. *(Re* **MARGOT**.) The voice of authority.

MAXINE. I can say, "Yes, I am, but it's early days."

TONY. Is that true?

MAXINE. Yes.

TONY. Well, tell. Come on, you know you want to show off.

MAXINE. Okay. A woman – she's married – is supposed to meet her lover at a hotel, but she knows her husband's hired a private detective to follow her. So, when she arrives, she doesn't go straight up to the room, she goes to the bar and orders a drink. She wants to figure out who the private detective is. A man comes in, orders something. The wife notices him looking at her. He's the only man in the bar. She starts a conversation with him. She's making sure the detective knows she's spotted him, if she's spotted him, he'll have to give up the chase. They chat. The man leaves the bar, leaves the hotel, the wife goes up to the room. Next day her husband tells her his private detective saw her go into that room. The wife is stunned. The man she talked to in the bar didn't follow her up to the room, she's certain.

> (*To* **TONY**.)

How did she get it so wrong?

TONY. (*Stumped.*) Uhm –

MARGOT. The private detective was a woman.

> (**TONY** *and* **MAXINE** *look at* **MARGOT**.)

The wife assumed the private detective was a man because private detectives are always men. She noticed a *man* in the bar looking at her, but she didn't notice if any of the women were.

TONY. Is that it?

MAXINE. It will be now. Do we have time for one more?

TONY. A quick one.

MARGOT. Me too.

> (**TONY** *takes their empty glasses and mixes drinks.*)

TONY. Oh, darling, I can't seem to find my latchkey. May I borrow yours?

MARGOT. Mine?

TONY. Yes.

MARGOT. What if I go out?

TONY. I thought you were staying in this evening.

MARGOT. Why should I? The two of you are going to be out and about, at the BBC, having a late supper at the Savoy Grill.

MAXINE. Join us. Meet us at the Savoy. We'll get tight as a drum.

MARGOT. You're sweet, but no. Mr. Pottifer always manages to put his hands where he shouldn't, no matter how far away we're seated.

MAXINE. What will you do instead, go to a movie?

TONY. I supposed you were going to listen to Maxine's interview.

MARGOT. *(To* **MAXINE.***)* Would you like me to?

MAXINE. Be nice to know how I come across.

MARGOT. Your voice can get brittle sometimes.

MAXINE. When?

MARGOT. When you're nervous.

MAXINE. I'm never nervous.

> *(To* **TONY.***)*

Give me a shot of bourbon just before they turn on the microphone.

> *(***TONY*** *gives* **MAXINE** *her drink and [intentionally] spills it on her dress.)*

Oh!

MARGOT. Tony!

TONY. Sorry. I'm a clod, I / know –

MAXINE. It's okay, / it's –

MARGOT. / No, that'll leave a stain.

MAXINE. It's a radio interview, no one's going to see it.

MARGOT. You reek of bourbon. The interviewer will think you're a dipsomaniac. I've got some remover in my basket.

> (**MARGOT** *picks up the mending basket and puts it on the desk. She opens it and searches, taking out a pair of stockings.*)

TONY. Is the remover the little brown bottle?

MARGOT. Yes, it's in here somewhere.

> (**MARGOT** *takes out a pair of scissors and puts them on the desk.*)

TONY. Actually, I think it's in the bedroom.

MARGOT. Is it?

> (*To* **MAXINE.**)

Come on, I'll get it out.

> (**MARGOT** *takes* **MAXINE** *into the bedroom.*)
>
> (*The moment they are out of sight –*)
>
> (**TONY** *takes the key from Margot's handbag and opens the front door.*)
>
> (*We hear* **MARGOT** *and* **MAXINE** *offstage:*)

MAXINE. *(Offstage.)* What's in the remover?

MARGOT. *(Offstage.)* Acid, naturally.

MAXINE. *(Offstage.)* Oh, good, make sure it burns an enormous hole.

(**TONY** *slips the key under the fifth step stair carpet, then re-enters, closing the front door.*)

MARGOT. *(Offstage.)* It'd be easier if you took it off.

MAXINE. *(Offstage.)* I suspected you had ulterior motives.

MARGOT. *(Offstage. Laughs.)* Stop it!

MAXINE. *(Offstage. Laughs.)* You're the one who said "Take off your dress"!

MARGOT. *(Offstage. Still laughing.)* I'm talking about the spot!

MAXINE. *(Offstage. Still laughing.)* "Out, out damn'd spot!"

(**TONY** *takes his raincoat from the coat rack and crosses to the desk.*)

(**MARGOT** *and* **MAXINE** *enter.*)

(**TONY** *takes his gloves from the raincoat pocket. His own key drops out of a glove onto the desk.* **TONY** *holds up his key.*)

TONY. Look. My latchkey. It was in my glove the whole time.

MAXINE. Mystery solved.

(**TONY** *puts his key back in his raincoat pocket.*)

TONY. Now we've got to run.

MAXINE. The studio isn't far, is it?

TONY. No, just across the park, a three minute walk if we're brisk.

MAXINE. Anything you want me to slip into the interview?

MARGOT.   What, like "And a fond hullo to Margot Wendice, famous shut-in"? Find a way to sneak "button mushrooms" into one of your answers.

MAXINE. Button mushrooms.

MARGOT. Bet a quid?

MAXINE. You're on.

> (**MAXINE** *downs her drink.*)

> (**TONY** *puts on his raincoat, opens the front door, and kisses* **MARGOT** *on the cheek.*)

TONY. Good-night, darling.

MARGOT. Have fun.

> (**MAXINE**, *having seen the passionless kiss husband has given wife, turns to* **MARGOT**.)

MAXINE. Night, sweets.

> (**MAXINE** *kisses* **MARGOT** *on the lips. The kiss is held a nanosecond longer than necessary, leaving* **MARGOT** *a little shaken as –*)

> (**MAXINE** *whisks up her fur and sweeps off.*)

> (**TONY** *follows her off.*)

MARGOT. *(Shaken, calls offstage.)* Be brilliant!

> (*Sound of street door opening and closing.*)

> (**MARGOT** *remains still for a moment. Then she closes the front door.*)

> (*She turns to look at her living room. Her expression falters.*)

(We hear a church clock outside chime the half hour.)

(**MARGOT** *goes to the drinks table and pours a large whiskey.)*

(**MARGOT** *takes her drink and exits to the bedroom as –)*

(Lights fade.)

(In the black, we hear the church clock outside chime eight o'clock. Then we hear the BBC interview over the radio. [Full transcript at the back of the script.])

BBC INTERVIEWER. *(Over radio.) This evening our guest is Maxine Hadley, author of* Your Death Is Necessary. *It's being advertised as a thriller. Is it a thriller?*

MAXINE. *(Over radio.) Well, my publishers call it a thriller.*

BBC INTERVIEWER. *(Over radio.) It certainly looks like a thriller from the dust jacket.*

MAXINE. *(Over radio.) Lurid, isn't it?*

BBC INTERVIEWER. *(Over radio.) I suppose the first thing, really, is to define what we're talking about when we use the word "thriller."*

MAXINE. *(Over radio.) I'd say they're novels that thrill.*

Scene Three

(The same.)

(Later that night.)

(Lights rise.)

(The living room is dark, but for moonlight.)

(Sound of rain.)

(The scissors are still on the desk.)

(The handbag is still on the table.)

(The radio interview, muted now, continues, coming from the bedroom.)

MAXINE. *(Over radio.) Wilkie Collins called his books sensation novels, because they caused the reader to feel the sensations of dread, horror, suspense. But I think all novels should have those sensations, at least to a degree.*

BBC INTERVIEWER. *(Over radio.) What's the difference between a thriller and a mystery?*

MAXINE. *(Over radio.) In a murder mystery, the question is something like who killed Lord Frumfry in the library? In a thriller, the questions are will this or that character commit murder, what's the killer after, will he kill again?*

(We hear a key in the front door.)

BBC INTERVIEWER. *(Over radio.) And you've got to have a good villain.*

MAXINE. *(Over radio.) A good villain is essential.*

(The front door opens.)

(Light pours in, silhouetting **LESGATE**.*)*

BBC INTERVIEWER. *(Over radio.)* Although, *in my own experience, I don't think I've ever encountered anyone who was an out and out villain.*

MAXINE. *(Over radio.) I have.*

BBC INTERVIEWER. *(Over radio.) Really?*

MAXINE. *(Over radio.) Oh, yes. So have you, you just didn't know it.*

BBC INTERVIEWER. *(Over radio.) You may be right there.*

*(***LESGATE** *enters.)*

(He closes the front door, softly.)

(He wears a raincoat, kid gloves, and tan scarf with tassels. He surveys the room. He takes off his scarf and ties two knots in it.)

So, then, what are the essential elements of a good thriller?

MAXINE. *(Over radio.) Well, it should have at least one murder. Preferably more. In ascending levels of violence.*

*(***LESGATE** *puts the knotted scarf into his raincoat pocket and moves to the desk.)*

There must be suspense. Questions must be posed. Events foreshadowed. And of course the stakes must be high.

*(***LESGATE** *looks at the telephone, then at his watch. He takes a flask from his pocket and drinks.)*

BBC INTERVIEWER. *(Over radio.) High enough for one of the characters to commit murder, I should think.*

MAXINE. *(Over radio.) Yes, motive is everything, even if the murder is unplanned.*

(The bedroom door opens.)

(A light falls across the living room floor.)

*(**LESGATE** starts. He backs away into the shadows.)*

*(**MARGOT** enters, in her nightgown. She holds her empty cocktail glass and starts to the drinks table when –)*

*(She sees **LESGATE**, drops the glass. It breaks.)*

MARGOT. Who are you? What are you doing here?

(Pause.)

LESGATE. I'm afraid I've come to kill you.

MARGOT. …Is this a joke?

LESGATE. Actually, it isn't, no. I…I was paid five thousand pounds to murder you. But / I –

*(**LESGATE** takes a step towards **MARGOT**.)*

MARGOT. / Don't come nearer!

LESGATE. Sorry… what I was going to say is: I don't have to go through with it. Killing you. I mean, I've *got* my money. *Your* money, actually.

MARGOT. My money?

LESGATE. The five thousand pounds you paid for that letter you never got back. The blackmail. Pretty neat trick, you must admit, getting you to pay for your own murder. The thing is it's all planned out to the minute. It's got to take place precisely at ten after eight.

MARGOT. Ten after eight?

LESGATE. Because of the alibi. Do you hear it? The radio?

MAXINE. *(Over radio.) I'm always more interested in the murderer than the victim.*

LESGATE. Don't you want to know who paid me?

MARGOT. *(After a beat.)* Who?

LESGATE. Yes, well, the price for that is ten thousand pounds. Isn't too much to find out who it is wants you dead, is it? Hm?

(**MARGOT** *reaches for the phone on the desk.*)

Don't touch that phone!

MARGOT. *(Freezes.)* The police are just around the corner.

LESGATE. *(An ugly hiss.)* Don't. Touch it.

(The phone rings.)

(**LESGATE** *and* **MARGOT** *look at the phone. They look at each other.*)

(The phone rings again.)

(**MARGOT** *grabs up the receiver.*)

(**LESGATE** *pulls out his scarf and lunges at* **MARGOT.**)

(He throws the scarf over her head and draws it back sharply against her throat.)

(**MARGOT** *drops the phone.*)

(**MARGOT**'s *hands catch hold of the scarf and try to tear it away. They struggle, then* **LESGATE** *winds the scarf around her neck.*)

(**MARGOT** *gropes for the scissors. She grabs them and drives them into* **LESGATE**'s *back.*)

(**LESGATE** *cries out, then falls on the floor, on his back.*)

(**MARGOT** *tears the scarf away from her throat and grabs up the telephone.*)

MARGOT. *(Short gasps.)* Police! Get the police! – Tony? Tony, come home! Come home, now, quickly, please! A man attacked me! He tried to strangle me. – No, he's dead.

(*Long pause.*)

Tony? Tony, are you still there? – Yes? Yes, I'm listening. – I won't, I won't touch anything. I won't call anyone – I promise, only be quick!

(**MARGOT** *hangs up. She crosses to the drinks table.*)

(*We hear the crunch of broken crystal. She has stepped on the shattered cocktail glass.*)

(**MARGOT** *takes another glass and pours a large whiskey, drinks half of it down in one gulp, then finishes off the rest. She puts the glass on the drinks table.*)

(**MARGOT** *moves to the French doors, keeping her eyes on* **LESGATE** *as though she fears he will come back to life and attack her.*)

(**MARGOT** *opens the French doors and exits to the garden.*)

(*We hear a rise in the sound of rain and traffic.*)

(*Sound of the church clock chiming the quarter hour.*)

(Sound of street door opening.)

(Running footsteps in passage outside apartment.)

(Sound of key in front door lock.)

(The front door opens.)

*(**TONY** enters, wearing his raincoat, holding his key.)*

*(**TONY** takes in the scene, puts the key into his raincoat pocket.)*

*(He crosses to **LESGATE**'s body. He kneels, turns him over and sees the scissors in his back. He is just beginning to search **LESGATE**'s pockets when –)*

*(**MARGOT** enters through the French doors.)*

*(**TONY** immediately stands as **MARGOT** rushes into his arms.)*

Oh, Tony!

TONY. It's all right, it'll be all right. What happened?

MARGOT. He tried to strangle me. He got something around my throat, it felt like a stocking.

TONY. But the scissors –

MARGOT. I stabbed him.

TONY. The blades went right through.

MARGOT. Cover him, can't you?

TONY. Yes, of course.

*(**TONY** crosses to the window seat, opens it and takes out a blanket. He covers **LESGATE**'s body.)*

(MARGOT goes to her handbag and opens it.)

Did he –?

(TONY sees MARGOT fishing around inside her handbag.)

What are you doing?

MARGOT. Looking for an aspirin. My head's pounding.

TONY. *(Hurries to take the handbag from her.)* Here, let me.

(TONY opens her purse, gets bottle, shakes out an aspirin.)

I'll get you some water.

(TONY pours a glass of water and gives it to MARGOT. She takes it.)

He must have broken in. I wonder what he was after.

MARGOT. When will the police get here?

TONY. Did you call them?

MARGOT. No. You told me not to speak to anyone. Hadn't you better call them now?

TONY. *(Thinking.)* In a minute, in a minute.

MARGOT. I'll get dressed.

TONY. Why?

MARGOT. They'll want to talk to me.

TONY. Right, yes...

(MARGOT starts to the bedroom, then stops, focuses on the radio. We can hear the interview at a lower volume.)

MARGOT. Maxine's still at the studio.

TONY. *(Nods, distracted.)* I told them to tell her there was a minor emergency.

MARGOT. ...Tony?

TONY. Hm?

MARGOT. Why did you phone?

TONY. ...I'll tell you about that later. You said he used a stocking?

MARGOT. I think it was a stocking, or a scarf. Isn't it there?

TONY. No. But I expect the police will find it. Go and change. I'll phone them right away.

> (**MARGOT** *nods, then exits into the bedroom, closing the door.*)

> (**TONY** *hurries to* **LESGATE**'s *body and resumes his frantic search. Finally, he finds the key in Lesgate's trouser pocket. He takes the key and puts it in Margot's handbag.*)

> (**TONY** *looks around, then leans down and picks up Lesgate's scarf. He starts to untie the knot. Then he stops. Thinks. He tightens the knot, goes to the phone and dials.*)

> *(Into phone.)*

Hello, Operator, give me the Maida Vale Police, quickly. Yes, hello. There's been a ghastly accident, a man's been killed. – Wendice. – 61a Charrington Gardens. – About ten minutes ago. He broke in and attacked my wife.

A burglar, so it seems. How long until you can get here? – Two minutes. Good. – No, we won't touch anything. Good-bye.

> (**TONY** *hangs up.*)

(A moment to think.)

(Then he goes into gear:)

(He opens the mending basket and finds two stockings. He holds up the scarf and the stockings, comparing them.)

(He stuffs Lesgate's scarf into his own raincoat pocket.)

(He ties two knots in one stocking and drops it under the desk.)

(He takes the other stocking to the coffee table. He picks up a magazine. He tears out three or four pages. He balls up the stocking, crumples the magazine pages around the stocking, then stuffs them all deep into the wastebasket.)

(He crosses back to **LESGATE**, *takes out his own wallet, and removes the letter from it. Using his handkerchief, he slips the letter into Lesgate's jacket pocket.)*

BBC INTERVIEWER. *(On radio.)* Do you think there's such a thing as a perfect murder?

MAXINE. *(On radio.)* Absolutely. On paper, I could plan a murder better than most people, but I doubt I could carry it out.

BBC INTERVIEWER. *(On radio.)* Really?

MAXINE. *(Over radio.)* Oh, I might be able to carry it out, but in stories things turn out as the author plans them to, in real life they don't. I'm sure I'd make some stupid mistake and not realize it until the end when I saw that everyone was looking at me.

(**MARGOT,** *now in slacks and a sweater, enters from the bedroom.*)

BBC INTERVIEWER. *(Over radio.) Can you give our listeners an example?*

MAXINE. *(Over radio.) Oh, let's see. A housewife makes dinner for her husband. Spaghetti with mushrooms. The husband eats the dinner and dies, apparently of a heart attack. As his body is being taken away, something falls from his trouser cuff. They test it and find it's full of poison. What fell out of his trouser cuff? A button mushroom.*

(*We hear the front door buzzer.*)

TONY. That'll be the police. Margot?

MARGOT. Yes?

TONY. Did he say anything?

(*Long pause.*)

MARGOT. No.

(**TONY** *takes that in.*)

(**TONY** *moves to open the front door.*)

(**MARGOT** *stares off, eyes red and wet as –*)

(*Fade to black.*)

End of Act One

ACT TWO

Scene One

(The same.)

(The next morning.)

(**TONY**, *in his dressing gown, is on the phone.*)

TONY. *(On phone.)* No, I'm sorry, my wife can't see anyone just now.

> (**MARGOT** *enters from the bedroom, fully dressed, wearing a turtleneck sweater that covers her bruises.*)

(On phone.) I'm afraid not, sorry, good-bye.

MARGOT. Who was that?

TONY. Another reporter.

MARGOT. How many is that now?

TONY. The fourth. So far.

> *(We hear the front door buzzer.)*

I'll get it.

> (**TONY** *opens the front door.*)

MAXINE. Where's Margot?

TONY. Here, come –

(**MAXINE** *hurries in, wearing gloves.* **TONY** *closes the front door.*)

(**MAXINE** *hugs* **MARGOT**. **MARGOT**'*s hands hover, unable to embrace* **MAXINE**. **MAXINE** *senses her resistance.*)

MAXINE. Did he hurt you?

TONY. Just some bruising. On her throat.

(**MARGOT** *hesitates, then loosens her turtleneck to reveal the purple bruises.*)

MAXINE. Jesus.

(**MAXINE** *makes a move towards* **MARGOT**, *but* **MARGOT** *pulls away.* **MAXINE**, *stung and confused, removes her gloves and sets them on the table.*)

Why didn't you tell me what happened?

TONY. Look, I / know –

MAXINE. / When they said it was a minor emergency, I figured it was something like a bathtub leak. Reading it in the papers this morning –

TONY. Yes, sorry, I should have phoned your hotel, but the police kept us rather busy last night. They didn't leave until past three. Would you like coffee? I can make some.

MAXINE. No. Thanks.

TONY. I'd, erm, best change. Keep Margot company, would you?

(**TONY** *exits to the bedroom, closes the door.*)

MAXINE. What's the matter?

MARGOT. Didn't you hear? I stuck a pair of scissors into a man last night. I'm a murderer now.

MAXINE. No, you're not. You defended yourself.

MARGOT. I did. Yes.

MAXINE. I'm proud of you.

MARGOT. Are you?

MAXINE. Of course I am. If you hadn't done what you did... The papers say it was a burglary.

MARGOT. Do they?

MAXINE. Well, isn't that what it was?

MARGOT. That's not what *he* said.

MAXINE. Who?

MARGOT. The man who attacked me.

MAXINE. ...He spoke to you?

MARGOT. Oh, yes.

MAXINE. What did he say?

MARGOT. He said... He said he'd been paid five thousand pounds to murder me.

MAXINE. What?

MARGOT. *(Nods.)* He said: "I've got my money. *Your* money, actually."

MAXINE. *(Putting it together.)* The five thousand pounds you paid for the letter?

MARGOT. *(Nods.)* He called it a neat trick, getting a person to pay for her own murder.

MAXINE. Who did he say sent him?

MARGOT. We never got that far. I was wondering if it might have been you.

MAXINE. I'm sorry?

MARGOT. I said you could have written those blackmail notes, and when you got the money, you could've used it to pay him to kill me.

MAXINE. Just why should I do that?

MARGOT. Revenge. For my breaking things off. It is one of your five reasons, isn't it? Revenge? And it's the sort of thing you think up, plotting how to murder people, working it out. He said the murder was planned, it was planned to take place at precisely ten after eight. It had to take place precisely then because the alibi was the radio.

MAXINE. Why would his alibi be the radio?

MARGOT. That's what I couldn't figure. But then I'm stupid. He didn't say it was *his* alibi. He said it was *the* alibi. It didn't hit me until I realized I could hear your voice. I'd tuned in just as I said I would. He had to kill me at that moment precisely because that was when you were on the talks program. An alibi of three million listeners.

MAXINE. Margot, / this –

MARGOT. / Then I thought about your letter that I couldn't destroy. It was so passionate, uncharacteristically so. I started to wonder if you'd written about us that way for a reason: so the letter couldn't help but be read as incriminating. No one reading a letter like that could think our friendship was innocent, not after you'd described it that way. It would be unmistakable that we'd been lovers. I'd have no choice but to buy it back, a boringly conventional woman like me, so fearful of scandal. You were right, five thousand pounds didn't make much of a difference to me. But it could make quite a difference to a struggling writer living in a sixth floor walkup.

    (Pause.)

MAXINE. Just so I've got this straight: I wrote a love letter so I could blackmail you for five thousand pounds, then used that five thousand pounds to have you killed.

MARGOT. Does it work?

MAXINE. It's good. May I steal it?

MARGOT. It's all yours. Even...

(*Laughs.*)

...even the blackmail notes I showed to you, you actually managed to make me give them back to you.

MAXINE. "Back" to me? What, you think I did that to cover my tracks?

MARGOT. Where are they now?

MAXINE. At my hotel.

MARGOT. And probably hard to find.

MAXINE. Do you know how crazy you sound?

MARGOT. (*Explodes.*) I killed a man last night!

MAXINE. (*Beat; careful.*) I know. Didn't think you had it in you. I see now that you do. What did the police think when you told them this man said he'd been paid to kill you?

MARGOT. I didn't tell the police.

MAXINE. Why not?

MARGOT. Because if I told them that, I'd have to tell them the rest, about the money, the letter, us.

MAXINE. Did you tell Tony?

MARGOT. The only person I've told is you.

MAXINE. Why?

MARGOT. To see how you'd react.

MAXINE. Are you satisfied?

MARGOT. Not really.

> *(We hear the front door buzzer.)*

TONY. *(Offstage.)* Margot? Can you get it?

MARGOT. *(Calls.)* I'd rather not right now!

> *(**TONY** enters from the bedroom, dressed.)*

TONY. ...I'll get it, then, shall I?

> *(**TONY** opens the front door.)*

> *(**INSPECTOR HUBBARD**, in a raincoat, stands there.)*

INSPECTOR HUBBARD. Mr. Wendice?

TONY. Yes.

INSPECTOR HUBBARD. My name's Hubbard. May I come in?

TONY. Yes, please.

> *(**INSPECTOR HUBBARD** enters. **TONY** closes the front door.)*

INSPECTOR HUBBARD. Mrs. Wendice. I'm Chief Inspector Hubbard.

TONY. Erm, Inspector, this is Miss Hadley. A friend of ours.

INSPECTOR HUBBARD. *Maxine* Hadley. You and Mr. Wendice were together last evening.

MAXINE. Yes.

INSPECTOR HUBBARD. Why was that?

MAXINE. Why was what?

INSPECTOR HUBBARD. Why were the two of you together?

TONY. Miss Hadley was being interviewed for a talks program at the BBC.

MAXINE. Mr. Wendice works for my publisher.

INSPECTOR HUBBARD. You're an author?

MARGOT. *(Pointed.)* Miss Hadley writes murder mysteries.

TONY. Erm, what can we do for you, Inspector? We gave your people all the necessary information last night.

INSPECTOR HUBBARD. Yes, I'm sure, but there are a few things I'd like to get firsthand.

(Re: raincoat.) May I...?

TONY. Of course.

> (**INPSECTOR HUBBARD** *takes off his raincoat and hangs it on the coat rack.*)

MAXINE. I should be going.

INSPECTOR HUBBARD. Oh, Miss Hadley, we may want to go over the odd detail with you later. Could you give me your address?

MAXINE. I'm staying at the Ritz.

INSPECTOR HUBBARD. *(Hands her his notebook and pencil.)* Write it there for me, would you? Room number, all that.

MAXINE. Okay.

INSPECTOR HUBBARD. Is this your first visit to London?

MAXINE. *(Writing.)* No, I used to live here.

INSPECTOR HUBBARD. For how long?

MAXINE. Three years.

INSPECTOR HUBBARD. Where?

MAXINE. Chelsea. Bywater Street.

INSPECTOR HUBBARD. Off the King's Road.

MAXINE. Yes.

INSPECTOR HUBBARD. That's just down from The Grape and Vine, isn't it?

MAXINE. If you say so.

INSPECTOR HUBBARD. When did you leave London?

MAXINE. A year ago.

> (**MAXINE** *hands the notebook and pencil back to* **INSPECTOR HUBBARD**.)

INSPECTOR HUBBARD. Thank you.

MAXINE. I, erm, may drop by later, if that's all right.

TONY. Yes, please do. I'll see you out.

MAXINE. No, I know the way.

> (**MAXINE** *opens the front door and exits.*)

TONY. Shall we sit?

INSPECTOR HUBBARD. Thank you. That was a very nasty experience you had last night, Mrs. Wendice.

TONY. Erm, do you know yet who the man was?

INSPECTOR HUBBARD. We're uncertain as to his real name. He had several. Pryce-Jones, Asprey, Waterhouse. The one he was going by recently was Lesgate. Had you seen him before, Mrs. Wendice?

MARGOT. No, of course not.

> (**INSPECTOR HUBBARD** *produces two snapshots and hands them to* **MARGOT**.)

INSPECTOR HUBBARD. Morgue photographs. Do you recognize him?

MARGOT. Yes.

INSPECTOR HUBBARD. You do? From...?

MARGOT. From last night.

INSPECTOR HUBBARD. No, I meant from before.

MARGOT. I told you I'd never seen him before.

INSPECTOR HUBBARD. Yes, of course, sorry. How about you, sir? Ever seen him?

> (**INSPECTOR HUBBARD** *hands* **TONY** *one photo.*)

TONY. No.

> (**INSPECTOR HUBBARD** *hands him the other photo.*)

No. At least... There is something familiar about him.

INSPECTOR HUBBARD. Oh?

TONY. Yes, but for whatever reason, I'm picturing him without a mustache.

INSPECTOR HUBBARD. So you think you might have met him?

TONY. Not *met* him, I'm sure of that. But...

INSPECTOR HUBBARD. Saw him?

TONY. Saw him, yes. I'm thinking it was at a railway station.

INSPECTOR HUBBARD. Mrs. Wendice, would you show me where you were last night when things happened?

> (**MARGOT** *stands and crosses to the bedroom door.*)

MARGOT. I was in our bedroom listening to the radio. I came in here to fix a drink.

INSPECTOR HUBBARD. Did you switch a light on?

MARGOT. No.

INSPECTOR HUBBARD. Would you show me where you were when he attacked you?

> (**MARGOT** *moves to the desk.*)

MARGOT. Here.

INSPECTOR HUBBARD. You said you went to fix yourself a drink.

> (**INSPECTOR HUBBARD** *moves to the drinks table to show that the desk is not in the same direction.*)

MARGOT. Erm, yes, but then I went to the desk.

INSPECTOR HUBBARD. *After* you fixed yourself a drink?

MARGOT. I didn't fix myself a drink.

INSPECTOR HUBBARD. Why not?

MARGOT. *(Hesitates.)* Because the phone rang.

INSPECTOR HUBBARD. This was your husband calling?

TONY. Yes.

INSPECTOR HUBBARD. Why were you calling your wife, sir?

MARGOT. Yes, *why did* you phone me?

TONY. I wanted to see if I could change your mind about going to supper.

> *(To* **INSPECTOR HUBBARD**.*)* Miss Hadley and I were going to the Savoy. My wife had elected not to join us.

> *(To* **MARGOT**.*)* I felt guilty about you spending the evening alone.

INSPECTOR HUBBARD. Right, then. You come in here, you go to the drinks table, the phone rings, you go over to the desk.

MARGOT. I went to the desk and I picked up the phone. That's when he attacked me.

INSPECTOR HUBBARD. Attacked you how?

MARGOT. He got something round my neck.

INSPECTOR HUBBARD. By "something" you mean...?

MARGOT. It felt like a silk stocking or a silk scarf.

INSPECTOR HUBBARD. What happened then?

MARGOT. He got the stocking or whatever it was around my neck and pushed me over the desk. I remember feeling for the scissors.

INSPECTOR HUBBARD. Were those scissors usually on the desk?

MARGOT. No, usually they're in that mending basket there, but I'd forgotten to put them away.

INSPECTOR HUBBARD. So, you forgot to put them away, but you remembered they were on the desk.

MARGOT. I didn't so much *remember*, I *felt* them.

INSPECTOR HUBBARD. So you felt for the scissors...?

MARGOT. I felt *around*, and...and my hands found the scissors, and I...I...I stabbed him with them.

INSPECTOR HUBBARD. Yes, I see. How do you suppose he got in?

MARGOT. Through the French doors there.

INSPECTOR HUBBARD. Why do you think that?

MARGOT. *(Unsure.)* Erm, because...

TONY. Because when I got back those doors were wide open.

INSPECTOR HUBBARD. Were they locked last night?

TONY. They were locked when Miss Hadley and I left for the studio.

INSPECTOR HUBBARD. Are you quite sure?

TONY. I always lock them when I leave the flat.

INSPECTOR HUBBARD. Then how did he get in?

TONY. We assume... well, he must have jimmied the lock.

INSPECTOR HUBBARD. The lock was carefully examined. It's quite undamaged. And there's no glass broken.

TONY. But that doesn't make sense.

(To **MARGOT**.) Darling, did you open the French doors last night?

MARGOT. Once, to get some air.

INSPECTOR HUBBARD. When was this?

MARGOT. After he attacked me.

INSPECTOR HUBBARD. Not before?

MARGOT. No.

INSPECTOR HUBBARD. Are you sure?

MARGOT. Yes.

INSPECTOR HUBBARD. Mrs. Wendice, why didn't you ring the police immediately after this happened?

MARGOT. I thought my husband would call them.

INSPECTOR HUBBARD. And it didn't occur to you to call for a doctor?

MARGOT. No.

INSPECTOR HUBBARD. Why not?

MARGOT. He was dead.

INSPECTOR HUBBARD. How did you know that?

MARGOT. It was obvious.

INSPECTOR HUBBARD. Did you feel his pulse?

MARGOT. No.

INSPECTOR HUBBARD. Did you check to see if he was breathing?

MARGOT. I didn't want to get near him, he'd just tried to kill me!

TONY. Inspector, the French doors. If the man didn't come in that way, how did he get in?

INSPECTOR HUBBARD. As a matter of fact, we're quite certain he came in by your front door.

MARGOT. But the front door is always locked.

TONY. Margot, did you open the door and forget to lock it after we'd gone?

MARGOT. No.

INSPECTOR HUBBARD. Are you quite certain you didn't?

MARGOT. I'm positive.

INSPECTOR HUBBARD. How many keys are there to the front door?

MARGOT. Only two. Mine was in my handbag and Tony had his with him.

TONY. That's right, I did.

INSPECTOR HUBBARD. Do you employ a charwoman?

MARGOT. Yes, but she hasn't got a key. I'm always in when she comes.

TONY. What makes you think he came in through the front door?

INSPECTOR HUBBARD. His shoes. It was raining last night. The ground was soaking wet. Muddy. If he'd come in through the French doors by way of the garden he'd have left footprints all over the floor. He didn't leave any because he wiped his shoes on the street door mat.

TONY. How do you know that?

INSPECTOR HUBBARD. It's a fairly new mat and some of its fibers came off on his shoes. Also, there was some tar on the mat and some of that got on his shoes as well. There's no question about it.

TONY. Wait a minute, I think I've got it. Do you remember that time when your handbag was stolen?

MARGOT. Yes.

TONY. Wasn't your key inside?

INSPECTOR HUBBARD. Hang on, I'd like to hear about this.

TONY. My wife lost a handbag at, where was it, Victoria Station? It was that weekend we went down to Portsmouth to see Peggy's new boat. We were in the station restaurant, and I said something like "That fellow there seems awfully interested in you." Remember?

MARGOT. I don't remember a man, but it was at Victoria where I lost my bag.

TONY. *(To* **INSPECTOR HUBBARD**.*)* That photograph you showed us, that was the man!

INSPECTOR HUBBARD. Did you get your bag back?

MARGOT. From the lost and found office about a week later.

INSPECTOR HUBBARD. Was anything missing?

MARGOT. Just a few pounds.

INSPECTOR HUBBARD. Nothing else was taken?

MARGOT. *(Catches.)* No.

INSPECTOR HUBBARD. No papers or letters?

MARGOT. No.

INSPECTOR HUBBARD. Was your latchkey in your handbag when you lost it?

MARGOT. Yes, but it was still there when it was returned.

TONY. Whoever stole the bag could have had the key copied. He could have had a duplicate key made and returned the original to the bag.

INSPECTOR HUBBARD. So he could have stolen your handbag, taken your key, copied it and used the duplicate key to open your front door.

MARGOT. Yes, he could have.

INSPECTOR HUBBARD. But of course he didn't.

TONY. Why not?

INSPECTOR HUBBARD. Because if he had, that duplicate key would still have been on him when he died. But no key was found when we went through his pockets.

MARGOT. No key?

TONY. So we're back where we started.

INSPECTOR HUBBARD. I'd like you both to make an official statement before the inquest. The station is only two minutes from here. Perhaps you could come now?

> (**MARGOT** *looks to* **TONY**, *hoping he will refuse.*)

TONY. If that's what we should do...

INSPECTOR HUBBARD. It won't take long. Mr. Wendice, I wonder if you might look out the street door. There was a small group of nosy parkers gathered when I came in. People read in their papers about a murder, and they line up like it's Madame Tussaud's.

TONY. Of course.

(**TONY** *opens the front door and exits, leaving the door open.*)

INSPECTOR HUBBARD. *(A beat, then: swift, hard.)* How much does he know?

MARGOT. What?

INSPECTOR HUBBARD. Your husband, how much does he know about you and your friend Miss Hadley. *(Takes out the letter.)* She wrote this letter to you from New York.

MARGOT. How did you get that?

INSPECTOR HUBBARD. It was found on the dead man, in one of his pockets. It makes for rather salacious reading. Any idea how it ended up on the body?

MARGOT. No.

INSPECTOR HUBBARD. When you lost your handbag at Victoria Station, did you lose this letter as well? Mrs. Wendice, your husband will be back any moment.

MARGOT. Yes, that letter was missing when I got back my handbag.

INSPECTOR HUBBARD. I asked you that before. You lied. Why?

MARGOT. I didn't want my husband to know! I –

(*We hear voices and footsteps from the hall.*)

(**INSPECTOR HUBBARD** *puts a finger to his lips and slips the letter back into his coat pocket.*)

(**TONY** *and* **MAXINE** *enter through the front door.* **TONY** *closes it.*)

INSPECTOR HUBBARD. Miss Hadley. Forget something?

MAXINE. I did, as a matter of fact. My gloves.

(MAXINE nods at her gloves on the table.)

INSPECTOR HUBBARD. Yes, I was wondering when you'd come back for them.

(To TONY.) How is it out there?

TONY. We've got a full blown mob. If we're to go to the station, you'll have to have your men disperse them.

INSPECTOR HUBBARD. It would be simpler to give them the slip by way of the garden. Unless they've gathered there too. Would you mind checking?

TONY. *(Knows INSPECTOR HUBBARD is trying to get rid of him)* Of course, Inspector.

> *(TONY exits through the French doors to the garden, leaving them open.)*

INSPECTOR HUBBARD. All right, Miss Hadley, I got rid of Mr. Wendice for you. You came back because you wanted to tell me something.

> *(INSPECTOR HUBBARD shows her the letter.)*

Is it about this?

MAXINE. How did...?

MARGOT. The police found it on Lesgate.

MAXINE. Lesgate?

INSPECTOR HUBBARD. The man Mrs. Wendice killed. A Mrs. Van Dorn let us into Lesgate's flat this morning. Behind a mirror we found five thousand pounds in sealed bank notes. We traced the serial numbers to your bank, Mrs. Wendice. You took out those same bank notes six months ago. Would you care to explain how Lesgate ended up with them?

MARGOT. I told you before, I never met any man named Lesgate!

INSPECTOR HUBBARD. Six months ago, he was calling himself Pryce-Jones and living above The Grape and Vine off Bywater Street.

(**MARGOT** *twigs on that, looks at* **MAXINE.**)

Did you happen to frequent The Grape and Vine when you were living there, Miss Hadley?

MAXINE. If The Grape and Vine was the closest purveyor of liquor, it's a good bet I did, but I didn't know a Pryce-Jones or Lesgate or whatever he was calling himself! All I know is someone was blackmailing Mrs. Wendice! After she lost that letter, she received two notes. This is one of them.

(**MAXINE** *takes out a blackmail note and gives it to* **INSPECTOR HUBBARD.**)

INSPECTOR HUBBARD. *(As he reads.)* Where's the other?

MAXINE. At my hotel somewhere, I couldn't find it.

INSPECTOR HUBBARD. How did *you* get them?

MAXINE. Mrs. Wendice showed them to me the day before yesterday.

INSPECTOR HUBBARD. *(Holds up note, to* **MARGOT.**) You paid the blackmailer five thousand pounds, didn't you?

MARGOT. Yes.

INSPECTOR HUBBARD. How did you get him the money?

MARGOT. I sent it to that address, like the note said to.

INSPECTOR HUBBARD. And you got back the letter?

MARGOT. I never got it back.

INSPECTOR HUBBARD. Is that why you met with him last night?

MARGOT. What?

INSPECTOR HUBBARD. To say you'd paid him the five thousand pounds he wanted, now give back the letter?

MARGOT. I didn't speak to him!

INSPECTOR HUBBARD. The evidence suggests you were in the middle of *entertaining* him.

MARGOT. This is / ridiculous.

INSPECTOR HUBBARD. / You say you came in here to make yourself a drink. But my men found two cocktail glasses. One was on the coffee table with your lipstick and fingerprints on it. The other was shattered on the floor next to the drinks table. It had been ground nearly to dust. We found shards of the same glass embedded in your slippers.

MARGOT. Yes, I stepped on it.

INSPECTOR HUBBARD. Did you intentionally crush that glass?

MARGOT. Why would I do that?

INSPECTOR HUBBARD. To make sure no fingerprints could be retrieved from it. So it wouldn't look like you and Lesgate were having drinks just before you killed him.

MARGOT. Why would I be having drinks with him in my nightgown?!

INSPECTOR HUBBARD. But you weren't wearing a nightgown.

> *(Consults notebook.)*

When the police arrived, you were dressed in a blouse and slacks.

MARGOT. I changed, that was after!

> *(**TONY** enters through the French doors.)*

Tony, tell him!

TONY. Darling, what's going on?

MARGOT. The inspector's trying to say I killed that man intentionally!

(*To* **INSPECTOR HUBBARD.**) It was self-defense!

INSPECTOR HUBBARD. Unfortunately, there were no witnesses, so we've only your word.

TONY. That's not true, I heard it over the telephone.

INSPECTOR HUBBARD. What exactly did you hear, Mr. Wendice? Did you hear anything that indicated a struggle was going on?

TONY. What I heard was consistent with my wife's explanation.

INSPECTOR HUBBARD. So all you really know is what your wife told you.

(*To* **MARGOT.**) You suggest that this man came to burgle your flat, but there's no evidence of a burglary. He didn't even have a bag to put things in. You told us he came in by way of the garden, but we know he came in by the front door.

MARGOT. But he can't have got in that way. That door was locked and there are only two keys. My husband had his with him and mine was in my handbag! Here!

(**MARGOT** *opens her handbag and takes out the key.*)

INSPECTOR HUBBARD. You could have let him in.

(*Beat.*)

MAXINE. You're not suggesting that Margot let him in herself.

INSPECTOR HUBBARD. It appears to be the only way he could have entered.

MARGOT. Don't you even believe I was attacked? How do you think I got these bruises on my throat?

INSPECTOR HUBBARD. You could have caused those bruises yourself. A silk stocking was found under the desk, with two knots tied in it.

MARGOT. That must have been the stocking he used.

INSPECTOR HUBBARD. We found its twin balled up inside some crumpled paper at the bottom of your wastebasket. The paper was torn out of a magazine that was on your coffee table. Can you explain why your attacker should do that?

MARGOT. ...No.

INSPECTOR HUBBARD. Those stockings were yours, weren't they?

MARGOT. No!

INSPECTOR HUBBARD. We know they were. One of the heels had been darned with some silk that didn't quite match. We found a reel of that silk in your mending basket.

MARGOT. That's because I was mending some...

(Rushes to mending basket and searches inside; doesn't find what she's looking for.)

There was a pair of stockings in here, I'm sure of it...!

INSPECTOR HUBBARD. Let's take a wide view, shall we? Lesgate stole your handbag at Victoria Station and discovered the letter in it. He decided to –

TONY. Hang on, what letter? What are you talking about?

INSPECTOR HUBBARD. The letter from Miss Hadley that Lesgate used to blackmail your wife. Mrs. Wendice paid him five thousand pounds for it, but he didn't return the letter.

(*To* **MARGOT**.) You arranged to meet him here last
night, which is why you...elected not to join Miss
Hadley and your husband at supper. You let Lesgate
in through the front door. You gave him a drink. You
argued. You killed him. The story that he was a burglar
who attacked you was sheer fabrication.

> (**MARGOT** *sees that* **TONY** *is staring at her,
> looking wounded.*)

MARGOT. (*Imploring.*) ...Tony –

> (**TONY** *holds up a finger: Stop.*)

TONY. (*Picks up phone.*) I'm telephoning our attorney. I've
heard of police deliberately planting clues to make sure
of a conviction, but / really!

INSPECTOR HUBBARD. / Mr. Wendice / –

TONY. / Your men were in here for hours last night! They
could easily have taken those stockings out of that
basket and done whatever they wanted with them.
They probably wiped the, the fella's shoes on the front
door mat as well!

INSPECTOR HUBBARD. Mrs. Wendice, I must advise you
anything you say –

MARGOT. He said he'd been paid to murder me!

> (*Pause.*)

INSPECTOR HUBBARD. Could you repeat that, please?

MARGOT. Lesgate, the man who... whoever he was, he
said he'd been paid five thousand pounds to murder
me! He offered to tell me who it was paid him if I gave
him another ten thousand pounds!

INSPECTOR HUBBARD. "Another" ten thousand pounds?

MARGOT. He said the radio was the alibi, then he put that stocking 'round my neck to strangle me, and I stabbed him!

INSPECTOR HUBBARD. So, Lesgate never got the chance to tell you who paid him to kill you.

MARGOT. ...No.

INSPECTOR HUBBARD. Pity.

MARGOT. It's the truth! It's what / he –!

INSPECTOR HUBBARD. / Let's go quietly, shall we, Mrs. Wendice? Else I shall have to call for the constables.

> (**MARGOT** *stares at* **INSPECTOR HUBBARD**, *shell-shocked. Then she nods, and, like a sleepwalker, starts to the French doors.*)

MAXINE. Margot. Your handbag.

> (**MARGOT** *stops.*)

> (**MAXINE** *takes the handbag to* **MARGOT** *and places it in her hands.*)

> (**MARGOT** *exits through the French doors to the garden.*)

> (**MAXINE** *follows.*)

INSPECTOR HUBBARD. Mr. Wendice?

TONY. Hm?

INSPECTOR HUBBARD. Will you be joining...?

TONY. Of course. Yes.

INSPECTOR HUBBARD. Ah. Just wondered.

> (**INSPECTOR HUBBARD** *exits.*)

*(**TONY** looks around the room, in complete control of the situation.)*

(Lights to black.)

End of Scene One

(In the black we hear:)

(A BBC news report fades in.)

BBC NEWSREADER. *(On radio.) ...The Home Secretary is at this hour deciding if there are sufficient grounds to justify a reprieve for Mrs. Margot Wendice. At the Old Bailey last November, Mrs. Wendice was found guilty of murder and sentenced to death. The trial, which featured lurid revelations regarding Mrs. Wendice and a close female friend, was notable for the accused's claim that the murdered man had been paid to kill her by a person or persons unknown. The jury returned a verdict of guilty in under an hour.*

Scene Two

(The same.)

(A few months after Scene One.)

(Early afternoon.)

(Lights up.)

(We hear a key turn in the front door.)

*(**TONY** enters. He wears his raincoat. He holds his key. He puts the key in his raincoat pocket, then takes the raincoat off and hangs it on the coat rack.)*

(Phone rings.)

*(**TONY** picks up.)*

TONY. *(Into phone.)* Hullo – Yes? – Oh, Fitzgerald, yes, I'm glad you called. If your paper wants to publish the letter I shall have to ask for five hundred pounds. – Yes, it is a lot of money, but the cost of my wife's defense was very high. – Yes, well, how would you like *your* wife's dirty laundry read by millions of people? – Yes, think it over, only I'm going away the day after tomorrow. – South America. I may never come back.

(Front hall door buzzer.)

Excuse me, I shall have to ring you later.

*(**TONY** hangs up. He opens the front door.)*

*(**MAXINE**, looking pale, stands there.)*

Come in.

*(**MAXINE** enters. **TONY** closes the front door.)*

MAXINE. Have you heard anything?

TONY. Your timing is impeccable. She's at the Home Office. Our lawyer has taken her. He says the chances of the Home Secretary granting clemency are slim to none. I expect someone will call shortly with the decision.

MAXINE. Why didn't you go with her?

TONY. She wouldn't allow it. I wanted to go to the prison this morning to say good-bye, but she wouldn't see me.

MAXINE. She's bad at good-byes.

TONY. Have you seen or spoken to her?

MAXINE. We haven't said a word to each other since she was arrested.

TONY. I suppose you'll be going back to New York now. I must say, it's been admirable of you, staying on after the trial, through the appeals, right to the end.

MAXINE. I'm not much in demand at present.

TONY. Yes. Rough stuff, your book being pulled. I suppose I should say I'm sorry. All those copies they printed before the scandal hit, taken off to the warehouse to be pulped. Oh, I should've offered you a drink. Bourbon on the rocks?

MAXINE. Yeah, sure.

> (As **TONY** speaks, he chops ice with an ice pick, makes **MAXINE** a bourbon, and gives it to her.)

TONY. What will you do now? Write another thriller, or have you done with that? I doubt I'd know how to sell it to the reading public. Not that I'd have to. I'm out of a job too, you know.

MAXINE. Yes, but you don't have to worry about being comfortable. Not after tomorrow morning.

(**MAXINE** *takes out a cigarette.*)

But I am working on something right now, since you ask.

TONY. Is it a mystery?

MAXINE. Yes and no. I'm teasing out the plot, but I don't think some of it holds up. The story's about a woman who kills a man to get back a letter from him. Only she doesn't find it. Even though the police find it quick enough, in one of the dead man's pockets. If you had just killed a man to get a letter, wouldn't you go through every one of his pockets to find it? I know I would. Especially if my husband was hurrying home from the BBC and he was the person I was trying to keep the letter from. Yet she doesn't.

TONY. You're not taking into account panic.

MAXINE. Oh, I'm allowing for panic, confusion, the race against the clock. According to the police, she had the presence of mind amid all that to find a stocking, tie knots in it, then hide its mate. If she had the presence of mind to do all that, why didn't she have the presence of mind to find the letter?

> (**TONY** *uses the ice pick to chop more ice, then pours himself a whiskey.*)

> (**MAXINE** *takes out a box of matches.*)

Then there are the stockings. She comes up with the idea to make it look like Lesgate used one of her stockings to strangle her. But then she's got the matching stocking to deal with. She can't leave it in the mending basket, it's the matching stocking that proves the other stocking is hers. She should destroy it. But she doesn't. She hides it in the wastebasket. Badly. So badly the police couldn't possibly overlook it. When the simplest and by far fastest way to get rid of that stocking in an instant would have been to...?

TONY. What?

MAXINE. *(Strikes a match.)* Put a match to it. The stocking would have gone up in a flash. Poof.

TONY. Would it?

MAXINE. Any woman knows that. Men don't though.

TONY. *(Mirthless smile.)* No, I suppose we don't.

MAXINE. I want to show you something.

> (**MAXINE** *takes out a note and offers it to* **TONY**. **TONY** *takes it.)*

TONY. It's the blackmail note.

MAXINE. The second one. Margot gave both of them to me.

TONY. At the trial, you testified that you couldn't find the second one.

MAXINE. I lied. I kept thinking it was a clue, that it would lead to something. I even went to the address on it, 23 Newport Street –

TONY. So did the police. They turned up nothing.

MAXINE. I know, but I still figured I could find a use for it. And I have. My fingerprints are on that note. So are Margot's.

> (**MAXINE** *takes the note from* **TONY**.)

And now so are yours.

TONY. What do you plan to do with it?

MAXINE. Tell the police I found it in a pocket. My fingerprints and Margot's are on it because she showed it to me. Both of us testified to that. But your fingerprints are on the blackmail note because...

TONY. Yes?

MAXINE. You wrote it, you sent it to Margot, you were the blackmailer, not Lesgate.

TONY. So. What's the deal? I go to the police and confess, or you'll give them that note with my prints on it? I'm not sure I see the advantage. If you give that note to the police, you implicate me. If I confess to the police, *I* implicate *myself.* Either way, I lose.

MAXINE. That isn't the deal.

TONY. What is it, then?

MAXINE. I give this note to the police, or you give me half of Margot's money.

TONY. *(After a beat.)* Oh.

MAXINE. As you said, my book's rotting in a warehouse waiting to be pulped. No respectable publisher will give me a tumble now, not after that trial. Oh, I might be able to write under a pen name, in a few years, but not for the kind of money I would have made if *Your Death is Necessary* had been a best seller. And it would have been a best seller.

TONY. Would have been, yes.

MAXINE. So, you see, I could use a bit of money about now.

TONY. Yes, but for you to get that money, *I* have to get that money, which means Margot has to be executed.

MAXINE. She does, yes.

>   *(Beat.)*

But do you know what I find interesting? You're not arguing the point. You're not saying you didn't hire Lesgate to kill Margot.

TONY. I don't think it necessary. As far as I can tell, you've ginned-up the same hysterical story Margot told when she was arrested, only with me as the villain, instead of you. The police didn't believe it then, neither did the jury.

MAXINE. No, they thought it was a desperate ploy by an unstable woman.

TONY. More to the point, there was no evidence to back it up.

MAXINE. There is now.

>(**MAXINE** *holds up the note.*)

>(**TONY** *goes very cold. We realize he's holding the ice pick.*)

>(*Sound of front door buzzer.*)

>(*Beat.*)

>(**TONY** *puts down the ice pick and moves to the front door.*)

>(**MAXINE** *puts the note in her pocket.*)

>(**TONY** *opens the front door.*)

>(**INSPECTOR HUBBARD**, *in his raincoat, stands there.*)

TONY. Inspector.

INSPECTOR HUBBARD. Mr. Wendice. Sorry to disturb you. May I come in?

>(**TONY** *nods.*)

>(**INSPECTOR HUBBARD** *enters, closes the door.*)

>(*As if surprised.*) Miss Hadley.

MAXINE. Inspector.

TONY. Maxine, tell Inspector Hubbard about the blackmail note.

INSPECTOR HUBBARD. Blackmail note?

TONY. Yes, show it to the inspector, will you?

> (**MAXINE** *glares at* **TONY**. *Then she takes the note from her pocket and* **TONY** *swiftly takes it from her.*)

Oh, dear. Now I've got my fingerprints on it. Sorry.

INSPECTOR HUBBARD. How did you get this?

MAXINE. I found it.

INSPECTOR HUBBARD. When?

MAXINE. Today.

INSPECTOR HUBBARD. Where?

TONY. In a pocket. Isn't that what you said, Maxine?

INSPECTOR HUBBARD. You testified at the trial that you made a thorough search for that second note.

MAXINE. I thought I had.

INSPECTOR HUBBARD. But when you find it today, you come to show it to Mr. Wendice. I wouldn't have thought the two of you would be so chummy.

TONY. We're old friends regardless.

INSPECTOR HUBBARD. Yes. Artistic people.

> (**INSPECTOR HUBBARD** *puts his raincoat on the coat rack next to* **TONY**'s *raincoat.*)

This note is very similar to the first note. I'm not sure what it adds.

MAXINE. Inspector, / I –

TONY. / Before you came, Inspector, Miss Hadley was spinning a story. Apparently I paid Lesgate to murder my wife because I was driven to homicidal fury by the relationship detailed in Miss Hadley's letter.

INSPECTOR HUBBARD. *(Disapprovingly.)* Yes, the letter.

MAXINE. The way all of you go on about "the letter," like little boys with a dirty magazine.

INSPECTOR HUBBARD. Some of it was rather graphic.

TONY. If certainly didn't help Margot's case.

MAXINE. Margot's case came down to three things: the letter, the stocking, and the key. Lesgate is supposed to have been blackmailing her because my letter was found in his pocket. But what if it was Tony who was blackmailing her? What if it was Tony who stole her handbag?

TONY. Why should I do that?

MAXINE. You wanted to find out who was writing to her. When it turned out it was me, you plotted your revenge.

TONY. But the letter was found in *Lesgate's* pocket.

MAXINE. You could have planted it on him.

TONY. When did I do this?

MAXINE. After you returned from the studio and before the police arrived.

TONY. And how does my revenge plot fit into this?

MAXINE. Oh, the revenge plot was the *original* plot. Lesgate was supposed to murder Margot.

TONY. And how did I persuade Lesgate to commit this murder he didn't commit?

MAXINE. With the five thousand pounds Margot paid for the letter you didn't return.

TONY. I see. Right, so, that's the letter. What about the key? *(To* **INSPECTOR HUBBARD**.*)* Miss Hadley does this for a living.

MAXINE. You told Lesgate you'd hide your key outside the flat. Above the door or under a pot, somewhere. Lesgate let himself in, then when you phoned / from –

INSPECTOR HUBBARD. / Miss Hadley, if Lesgate had used Mr. Wendice's key, it would still have been on him when he died. Besides, how did Mr. Wendice get in when he returned?

MAXINE. Margot could have let Tony in.

INSPECTOR HUBBARD. But Mrs. Wendice *didn't* let her husband in. He let himself in with his own key. Both of them testified to that.

TONY. Your move, Max.

MAXINE. Lesgate could have taken the key from wherever Tony hid it, unlocked the door, then returned it to its hiding place before he came in.

TONY. It all sounds very involved, I must have been planning this for years.

MAXINE. *One* year. Since you discovered Margot and I were lovers.

TONY. Maxine, I'm going to say something no one was ever supposed to know. When I came back here that night, I found Margot kneeling beside Lesgate's body, going through his pockets. She kept saying he had something of hers. A letter. She was hysterical. I had to calm her down, so I pulled her away from the body, which is when the police arrived. That's why she didn't retrieve the letter.

MAXINE. And you're telling this story just now?

TONY. I seem to be.

(To **INSPECTOR HUBBARD.***)* Inspector, I suppose I've committed a crime, admitting that.

INSPECTOR HUBBARD. All this has been out of my hands for months now. There's been a trial and an appeal and now the Home Office...

MAXINE. What about the Home Office?

TONY. Do you know if there's been a decision?

INSPECTOR HUBBARD. It's why I came. The Home Secretary has denied her request. The hanging will go forward tomorrow morning.

(To **TONY.***)* I'm very sorry, sir.

(Beat.)

(Then to **MAXINE.***)* May I walk you out?

MAXINE. You've been very clever, Tony. You plot like a master, and you improvise brilliantly. But you have made one mistake. Just now. What will happen when Margot hears about this?

TONY. About...?

MAXINE. Your story. Margot tearing through Lesgate's pockets, trying to find the letter.

TONY. She'll deny it.

MAXINE. She'll change her will. You'll have done it all for nothing.

> *(***MAXINE*** exits through the front door, closing it behind her.)*

TONY. Do you think they'll let her?

INSPECTOR HUBBARD. Let...?

TONY. Let Maxine see Margot. Can she be kept from visiting her in prison? I don't want my wife to be made upset.

INSPECTOR HUBBARD. Your wife isn't at the prison. She's likely to have just left the Home Office.

TONY. Oh, yes, right. But once she's back...

INSPECTOR HUBBARD. Tell you what: I'll ring up the warden and put a word in his ear. Stop Miss Hadley from making a scene.

TONY. *(Greatly relieved.)* Thank you, Inspector. You're very kind.

INSPECTOR HUBBARD. Not at all, sir. Oh, by the way, there are items belonging to Mrs. Wendice at the police station. Her gloves, handbag. You're to come and collect them today.

TONY. *(Annoyed.)* Can't they be sent here?

INSPECTOR HUBBARD. I'm afraid not. They have to be signed for in front of the Desk Sergeant.

TONY. Must it be today?

INSPECTOR HUBBARD. I'm afraid so, sir.

> **(INSPECTOR HUBBARD** *stoops down and appears to pick up something from the carpet beneath his raincoat.)*

Is this yours?

TONY. What is it?

INSPECTOR HUBBARD. Somebody's latchkey. It was lying on the floor, just here.

> **(TONY** *takes up his raincoat and feels in the pockets. He takes out his key and holds it up.)*

TONY. No. I've got mine here.

> **(TONY** *puts his key back into his raincoat pocket and puts his raincoat back on the coat rack.)*

INSPECTOR HUBBARD. Must be mine, then.

> (**INSPECTOR HUBBARD** *picks up his own raincoat, feels in pocket.*)

Yes, it is. It must have dropped out of my pocket. There's a small hole here. That's the trouble with those keys, they're all alike.

> (**INSPECTOR HUBBARD** *puts the key into his raincoat pocket. Then, while Tony is looking the other way, he switches his raincoat for Tony's raincoat. Inspector Hubbard's raincoat is now hanging on the coat rack.*)

Good-bye, Mr. Wendice. I don't suppose we shall meet again.

TONY. No. I suppose not. Again, thank you.

INSPECTOR HUBBARD. Yes, sir. I'll see myself out.

> (**INSPECTOR HUBBARD** *exits through the front door, closing it behind him.*)

> (**TONY** *waits a beat, then he crosses to the drinks table and pours whiskey into a glass and drinks it down.*)

> (**TONY** *picks up the phone and dials.*)

TONY. *(Into phone.)* Hullo, Fitzgerald? – Tony Wendice. – You have, eh? Well, I'm afraid the price has gone up. – I want one thousand pounds. – I know what I said earlier, but I'm raising it. I want your answer now, yes or no. – I thought you'd see reason.

> (*We hear the front door buzzer.*)

(Into phone.) Send the cheque in care of my attorney. He'll see the letter's delivered into your grubby little hands.

> (*Front door buzzer again.*)

(Into phone.) Yes, you too, good-bye.

> *(Sound of knocking, fast, urgent.)*

> *(The front door buzzer again, more insistent.)*

> *(**TONY** opens the front door.)*

> *(**MARGOT** hurries in, dressed in the same clothes she was wearing at the end of the previous scene. Her hair is wild, her face red, she's out of breath.)*

> *(**TONY** closes the door, stunned. Stares at her.)*

> *(Pause.)*

MARGOT. May I have some water?

> *(**TONY** continues to stare at her.)*

Please?

> *(**TONY** comes to, pours a glass of water, gives it to her. She drinks.)*

We were at the Home Office. They'd taken me there from my cell just after breakfast. I was kept in a room while they discussed the case. I sat there, thinking "They're not going to hang me tomorrow, they can't possibly. The Home Secretary won't allow it." Then the door opened, and they told me to come in. My solicitor wouldn't look at me. The Home Secretary was very brisk, very efficient. "Clemency denied." But I suppose that was too efficient because he added that only a brazen woman would have the nerve to request clemency after such a sordid trial, called me wanton, a degenerate.

Then it was over. My solicitor still refused to look at me. They took me back to the car. I got in the backseat.

There were only two guards, one in front to drive, the other in the back with me.

"They're going to hang me tomorrow. They're going to hang me and no one will help."

And then I noticed...the door was unlocked. They have no problem believing a woman's capable of committing murder in cold blood but not that she'd try to escape when she's to be hanged the next morning.

The car pulled away and started back to the prison. The streets were crowded. Traffic. "They're going to hang me tomorrow, they're going to hang me..."

I kept looking at the lock on the door, thinking one of them's got to notice, the guard sitting next to me will see, he'll reach over and lock it. But he didn't.

We stopped at a light. Regent's Park.

It was my only chance. I grabbed the door handle, pulled. And I ran, ran across the park.

TONY. Why in God's name did you come here?

MARGOT. Where else could I go? Please, for God's sake you've got to help me!

> (*TONY continues to stare at* **MARGOT**.)

Tony, say some –

> (*The phone rings.*)

> (**MARGOT** *and* **TONY** *look at the phone.*)

> (*It rings again.*)

> (**TONY** *looks at* **MARGOT**, *then takes a step towards the phone.*)

> (**MARGOT** *hurries to him, stops his hand from picking it up.*)

What if it's the police?

(**TONY** *puts a finger to his lips, picks up the phone. Answers.*)

TONY. *(Into phone.)* Hello. – Yes, sergeant, the inspector told me. Is it really necessary that I come pick them up today? – No, no, I'll be right there. –

(Hangs up.)

That was the police station. They have your handbag and other things to be picked up, they want me to come get them.

MARGOT. They didn't say anything about me?

TONY. *(Thinking.)* It appears word hasn't reached them yet.

MARGOT. Tony –

TONY. I'm improvising.

(Decides.)

We've got to get you away. We'll get you out of the country. The car's in the garage at the corner. I'll bring it round and drive us to Portsmouth. Peggy's boat is docked there.

MARGOT. How are we to manage a fifty-five-foot yacht?

TONY. Peggy has a captain. We'll pay him however much he wants. If the police ask, he can pretend he didn't know who we were.

MARGOT. But, / Tony –

TONY. / Darling, it's our only chance, they are going to hang you tomorrow! Now, I'm going to go and bring round the car. It shouldn't take more than five minutes.

MARGOT. Shouldn't I go with you?

TONY. No, you might be seen. Stay here. Don't answer the phone, don't answer the door. Promise?

MARGOT. I won't.

> (**TONY** *picks up Inspector Hubbard's raincoat from the coat rack and exits through the front door, closing it behind him.*)

> (**MARGOT** *paces, tense, nervous, frightened as she hears the sounds of cars passing, horns, a distant siren.*)

> (**MARGOT** *notices the two glasses* **TONY** *and* **MAXINE** *used. She picks one up.*)

> (**MARGOT** *sees the red lipstick on the rim.*)

> (*We hear the sound of a key in the front door.*)

> (**MARGOT** *starts, backs away behind the desk.*)

> (*The front door opens.*)

> (**MAXINE** *enters, leaving the door open.*)

> (**MARGOT** *sees her, gasps.*)

MAXINE. *(Sees* **MARGOT.***)* Margot? What the hell are you doing here?

MARGOT. You first.

MAXINE. I should think you'd be tired of asking house breakers what they're doing in your flat.

MARGOT. I ran away.

MAXINE. Does Tony know?

MARGOT. Tony's getting me out of the country. We're driving to Portsmouth. He's gone for the car. He'll be back in a minute.

MAXINE. My God.

> (*We hear footsteps approaching in the front hall.*)

MARGOT. Who's with you?

> (**INSPECTOR HUBBARD** *enters through the open front door. He holds a key in his hand, then pockets it carefully.*)

INSPECTOR HUBBARD. Mrs. Wendice?

MARGOT. I got away.

INSPECTOR HUBBARD. You did, eh? Well. Somebody will be given a very strong talking to. But never mind about that now.

> (**INSPECTOR HUBBARD** *closes the front door.*)

MARGOT. Aren't you going to arrest me?

INSPECTOR HUBBARD. You will be doing us all, especially yourself, a great deal of good by keeping quiet and behaving as you're told.

MAXINE. (*Takes* **MARGOT**'s *arm.*) Let's get you / into –

MARGOT. (*Pulls away.*) / No! Tell me what's going on! Especially as this isn't the first time you've been here today.

> (**MARGOT** *picks up the glass with the lipstick on it.*)

That's your color. The ice hasn't even melted yet. What were you doing?

MAXINE. Trying to save your life.

MARGOT. By having cocktails with my husband?

INSPECTOR HUBBARD. By trying to blackmail him. Not that it worked. Told you it wouldn't.

MAXINE. It was worth a try! I thought if I could get Tony's fingerprints on the blackmail note, he would pay me not to give it to the police. If he did that, it would be as good as a confession.

INSPECTOR HUBBARD. But he didn't, and it wasn't a confession.

MARGOT. What / do –?

> (/ *We hear the sound of footsteps in the front hall coming towards the flat.*)

INSPECTOR HUBBARD. *(Whispers.)* Quiet now!

> (**INSPECTOR HUBBARD** *turns down the lights.*)
>
> (*Sound of a key being inserted in the front door lock.*)
>
> (*Sound of key in lock continues. It's the sound of a key not fitting.*)
>
> (*Front door buzzer.*)
>
> (**MAXINE** *shakes her head at* **MARGOT**, *mouths "Don't".*)
>
> (*Door buzzer again.*)
>
> (*Sound of knocking on front door.*)
>
> (*Sound of knocking more urgently.*)
>
> (*Sound of footsteps going away, then street door opening and closing.*)

MARGOT. Who was that?

INSPECTOR HUBBARD. That was your husband.

MARGOT. Tony? But...why couldn't he get in?

INSPECTOR HUBBARD. He hasn't got his key.

MARGOT. But he took his...

> (*Looks at where Tony's raincoat was.*)

...he took his raincoat, he always keeps his key in the pocket.

(*Suspicious.*) Why wouldn't you let me answer the door?

MAXINE. What did he say when he left?

MARGOT. He told me to keep out of sight, don't open the door, don't answer the phone.

MAXINE. Then he thinks you're just following his instructions.

INSPECTOR HUBBARD. Now he's gone to the police station where he knows your handbag is waiting, and in it, your key.

> (**INSPECTOR HUBBARD** *picks up the phone, dials.*)

(*Into phone.*) Hubbard here. – He's realized about his raincoat. – He came back and couldn't get in. He's probably on his way to the station now. Give Wendice those gloves and the handbag and make sure he sees the key inside the bag. Better make him check the contents and sign for it. If he wants his own key and raincoat, tell him I've gone to Glasgow. Call me back when he leaves the station.

> (**INSPECTOR HUBBARD** *hangs up the phone.*)

MARGOT. Why do you think Tony's gone to the police station?

INSPECTOR HUBBARD. Because he's realized he picked up the wrong coat with the wrong key.

MARGOT. I don't understand.

INSPECTOR HUBBARD. Mrs. Wendice, what I've got to tell you may come as a shock. We strongly suspect that your husband plotted to murder you.

MARGOT. *(Small voice.)* How long have you suspected this?

INSPECTOR HUBBARD. Miss Hadley came to me this morning with, what did you call it, a plot snag?

MAXINE. The key. Call it my writerly obsession with tying up loose ends. It always bothered me that no key was found on Lesgate's body. Not even a key to his flat. Most people carry a key on them. Why didn't the police find one on Lesgate? So I went to see the inspector.

INSPECTOR HUBBARD. Miss Hadley seemed to be accusing Scotland Yard of doing a poor job. Well, I couldn't let that stand, so I decided to search this flat one more time, to see if I could find Lesgate's key. It could have fallen out during the struggle and ended up somewhere we hadn't looked, in the gap between two floor planks, behind a baseboard. But first I had to gain access to the flat. So I went to the station, got your handbag and lifted the key.

MAXINE. Stole it.

INSPECTOR HUBBARD. Then I waited until Mr. Wendice had gone out this morning and tried to get in.

MARGOT. Tried?

INSPECTOR HUBBARD. I never got in. The key I'd stolen from your handbag didn't fit the lock.

MARGOT. Why? Has Tony changed the locks?

INSPECTOR HUBBARD. No.

MAXINE. It wasn't your key.

MARGOT. Where's *my* key then?

MAXINE. It took me just half an hour to find it.

> (**MAXINE** *opens the front door, steps into the hall and points to the fifth step of the staircase.*)

It was hidden under the fifth stair carpet in the entry hall.

INSPECTOR HUBBARD. Wendice told Lesgate that he would leave your key under the stair carpet and to return it to the same place when he left. But as Lesgate was killed, Wendice naturally assumed your key would still be in one of Lesgate's pockets. That was his mistake. Because Lesgate had done exactly what Miss Hadley suggested. He unlocked the front door, and then returned the key *before* he came in.

MARGOT. And it's been out there in the hall ever since?

MAXINE. It's still there.

> (**MAXINE** *closes the front door.*)

MARGOT. So the key Tony took out of Lesgate's pocket and put in my handbag was...

INSPECTOR HUBBARD. Lesgate's own key!

MAXINE. We took the key that was in your handbag to a Mrs. Van Dorn's this morning. It unlocked the door to Lesgate's flat.

MARGOT. *(After a beat.)* Does this mean I'm free?

INSPECTOR HUBBARD. Actually, no, this is all supposition.

MARGOT. What?

INSPECTOR HUBBARD. Yes, I'm afraid we've yet to prove any of this.

(Phone rings.)

(Picks up.)

(Listens.) – Right, start the ball rolling. *(Hangs up.)* Mr. Wendice just left the station with your handbag. He's on his way back.

MARGOT. Did he tell them I was here?

INSPECTOR HUBBARD. He's smarter than that. He knows if the police come bursting in, you'd know it was him who tipped us off and change your will first thing. When he returns, he'll try the key from your handbag. When that key doesn't fit, he'll realize his mistake, put two and two together and look under the stair carpet.

MARGOT. But if he doesn't get that key, you can't prove a thing.

INSPECTOR HUBBARD. True. But if he opens that door, we shall know everything.

(Sound of three thumps above.)

MARGOT. What's that?

INSPECTOR HUBBARD. My men upstairs. There are two up top and three on the street.

(Phone rings.)

*(**INSPECTOR HUBBARD** picks it up, listens.)*

Quiet now. He's returned.

(A long silence.)

MARGOT. *(Very quiet.)* What if you're lying.

MAXINE. What?

MARGOT. What if this, everything you've been saying is just to keep me here until more police come and arrest me.

INSPECTOR HUBBARD. There aren't more police coming to arrest / you...

MARGOT. / You said you've got men up top, men in the streets! Maybe this is all just another lie!

INSPECTOR HUBBARD.	**MAXINE.**
Mrs. Wendice –!	Margot, for Christ's sake!

(Sound of the street door opening and footsteps coming towards the front door.)

MAXINE. *(Continued.)* Shh!

(They all freeze.)

*(***MARGOT*** suddenly rushes to the drinks table and grabs the ice pick. She holds it like a weapon.)*

INSPECTOR HUBBARD.	**MAXINE.**
What do you think you're doing?	*(Continued.)* Margot, please!

MARGOT. *(Whispers.)* Do you want me to hang? Tony's driving me to Portsmouth!

MAXINE. *(Whispers.)* You'll never reach Portsmouth! He's probably planning on running a traffic light that'll make a constable stop the car! That or a road accident, the kind the driver survives and the passenger doesn't!

MARGOT. *(Whispers.)* No. No, Tony doesn't think that way. *You're* the one who thinks that way!

(Sound of a key being inserted into the lock of the front door. The key is not fitting.)

(Sound of the front door buzzer.)

(Whispers.)

I've got to open the door!

(Sound of the front door buzzer being pressed again, over and over.)

(MARGOT *starts for the front door.)*

TONY. *(Offstage.)* Margot!

MAXINE. Margot, don't!

TONY. *(Offstage.)* Margot, open the door!

MARGOT. Why should I trust you?

MAXINE. You...you know why.

(MARGOT *and* **MAXINE** *stare at each other.)*

(Sound of banging on the door.)

TONY. *(Offstage.)* Margot, it's Tony!

(Sound of pounding on the door.)

(MARGOT *slowly lowers the ice pick and drops it to the floor.)*

(Silence.)

(Sound of a key being inserted into the front door. We hear the lock turn, open.)

(The front door opens.)

(Light pours in.)

(TONY *enters with the Inspector's raincoat. He holds Margot's handbag in one hand, a key in the other. He's staring at the key which means he doesn't see –)*

(**MARGOT** *and* **MAXINE** *staring at him.*)

(*Now he looks up. He sees* **MARGOT** *and* **MAXINE**. *He sees* **INSPECTOR HUBBARD**.)

(**TONY** *looks at the key, realizing.*)

(**INSPECTOR HUBBARD** *picks up the phone and dials.*)

(**MAXINE** *opens the cigarette box, takes out a cigarette, lights it, takes a long draw.*)

(**MARGOT** *raises her hand for the cigarette.*)

(**MAXINE** *gives it to her.*)

(**MARGOT** *takes a long, luxurious draw of smoke and exhales it at* **TONY** *as –*)

(*Lights fade to black.*)

End of Play

BBC INTERVIEW OVER THE RADIO
FULL TRANSCRIPT

BBC INTERVIEWER. This evening our guest is Maxine Hadley, author of *Your Death Is Necessary*. It's being advertised as a thriller. Is it a thriller?

MAXINE. Well, my publishers call it a thriller.

BBC INTERVIEWER. It certainly looks like a thriller from the dust jacket.

MAXINE. Lurid, isn't it?

BBC INTERVIEWER. I suppose the first thing, really, is to define what we're talking about when we use the word "thriller."

MAXINE. I'd say they're novels that thrill.

BBC INTERVIEWER. Wilkie Collins called his books sensation novels.

MAXINE. Yes, he did. Because they caused the reader to feel the sensations of dread, horror, suspense. But I think all novels should have those sensations, at least to a degree.

BBC INTERVIEWER. What's the difference between a thriller and a mystery?

MAXINE. In a murder mystery, the question is something like who killed Lord Frumfry in the library? In a thriller, the questions are will this or that character commit murder, what's the killer after, will he kill again?

BBC INTERVIEWER. And you've got to have a good villain.

MAXINE. A good villain is essential.

BBC INTERVIEWER. Although, in my own experience, I don't think I've ever encountered anyone who was an out and out villain.

MAXINE. I have.

BBC INTERVIEWER. Really?

MAXINE. Oh, yes. So have you, you just didn't know it.

BBC INTERVIEWER. You may be right, there. So, then, what are the essential elements of a good thriller?

MAXINE. Well, it should have at least one murder. Preferably more. In ascending levels of violence. There must be suspense. Questions must be posed. Events foreshadowed. And of course the stakes must be high.

BBC INTERVIEWER. High enough for one of the characters to commit murder, I should think.

MAXINE. Yes, motive is everything, even if the murder is unplanned.

BBC INTERVIEWER. Is an unplanned murder really murder? Or is that what we call manslaughter?

MAXINE. That's a legal distinction. To my way of thinking, the difference between premeditated murder and, say, a murder of opportunity is a question of degree.

BBC INTERVIEWER. Opportunity, interesting.

MAXINE. Opportunity, circumstance, situation. Timing is everything.

BBC INTERVIEWER. What else is essential to a satisfying thriller?

MAXINE. There are so many things: Setting. Does the story take place in a penthouse or a country cottage or a row house? Period. Is it a contemporary thriller, with automobiles and airplanes, or does it take place in the land of Sherlock Holmes with hansom cabs and gaslight? There's a world of difference between a murderer who has access to telephones and taxicabs and one who's denied these modern conveniences.

BBC INTERVIEWER. Because they haven't been invented yet.

MAXINE. Yes, fingerprints, ballistics, photographs, all these are of endless use to the police. Less so, the novelist.

BBC INTERVIEWER. Which of your characters do you identify with in your fiction? The murderer, or the victim?

MAXINE. I'm always more interested in the murderer than the victim, that's where my sympathies lie. But then I'm a bit perverse.

BBC INTERVIEWER. Oh, I'm sure that's not the case.

MAXINE. No, I'm serious, my murderers are my protagonists, so I must identify with them, if I didn't it would be malpractice.

BBC INTERVIEWER. (*Laughs.*) Oh, now, come!

MAXINE. Shakespeare knew what his murderers were after, what they wanted, he had to, otherwise they wouldn't be so persuasive.

BBC INTERVIEWER. Richard the Third, for example.

MAXINE. Yes. Shakespeare knew. Doesn't mean Shakespeare killed kiddies in a tower. But it might mean he knew what it was like to want to.

BBC INTERVIEWER. A bit aggressive, that, isn't it?

MAXINE. Writing is an aggressive act. Writers take their anger, their frustration, their resentment and fury and turn it into machine gun bursts of words.

BBC INTERVIEWER. And if the machine gun bursts hit their mark, the writer makes a killing?

MAXINE. You like a metaphor, don't you?

BBC INTERVIEWER. Well, I was simply taking up / your –

MAXINE. / No, no, it's good, I'm going to borrow that.

BBC INTERVIEWER. But seriously, when a book's done, when you're finished shooting your bullets, is the anger, the resentment, the fury what you will...gone? Dissipated? Expiated?

MAXINE. For a time, until it builds up again.

BBC INTERVIEWER. Ah, the author as serial killer.

MAXINE. Very Jack the Ripper.

BBC INTERVIEWER. Or Jack the Writer.

MAXINE. Well, he did write letters, didn't he, to Scotland Yard, taunting the police. Just another frustrated artist.

BBC INTERVIEWER. What about the hero?

MAXINE. I tend not to write heroes. At least not in the conventional sense.

BBC INTERVIEWER. No strong jawed fellows, eh?

MAXINE. No, no strong jawed fellows.

BBC INTERVIEWER. What about strong jawed women?

MAXINE. I'm not sure I know what you mean.

BBC INTERVIEWER. A strong woman, be she heroine or murderer.

MAXINE. All one's characters have to be strong.

BBC INTERVIEWER. Point taken. How realistic do you think thrillers should be, for example, we read in the American press that they had another killing last week in New York. One of these men connected with that dock union man – what's his name?

MAXINE. Albert Anastasia?

BBC INTERVIEWER. Anastasia, yes. How's a killing like that arranged?

MAXINE. Very simply. You want me to describe how it's done?

BBC INTERVIEWER. Yes, please.

MAXINE. Well, first of all the syndicate has to decide if he must be killed, and they don't want to kill people.

DDC INTERVIFWER. They don't?

MAXINE. No. It's bad business.

BBC INTERVIEWER. I see.

MAXINE. So, when they make the decision they telephone to a couple of men in, say, Minneapolis, in a hardware store or something – a respectful business front. These men come along to New York and they're given their instructions and they're given a photograph of the man and told what's known about him. They're given guns...

BBC INTERVIEWER. In Minneapolis?

MAXINE. No, not in Minneapolis. After they get their instructions they're given guns. Now, these guns are not defaced in any way, but they are guns that have passed through so many hands that the present owners can never be traced. The company could only say the first purchaser. So, they go to where the man lives, and they get an apartment or a room across the street from him. They study him for days and days and days until they know just exactly when he goes out, and when he comes home, what he does. And when they're ready, they simply walk up to him and shoot him. They have to have a crash car – Bugsy Siegel was a great man for the crash car. The crash car is in case a police car should come down the street, and it accidentally on purpose smashes the police car.

BBC INTERVIEWER. Yes, I see what you mean.

MAXINE. So, they get away. They get back on the plane and go home, and that's all there is to it.

BBC INTERVIEWER. Back to your own writing. Do you like to write torture scenes?

MAXINE. I was brought up on thrillers of the kind where Bulldog Drummond gets in the grips of the villain and he suffers, either he's drugged or something happens to him. But I don't like to get too serious. I get tired of the fact that the hero in other people's thrillers gets a bang on the head with a revolver butt and he's perfectly happy afterwards – just a bump on his head – they recover too quickly. If you're banged on the head with a revolver butt, the first thing you do is vomit.

BBC INTERVIEWER. Oh, dear. I didn't know that. How do you develop your characters? I mean, it seems to me in your book, the character building, and to a considerable extent in the dialogue, which of course I think is some of the best dialogue written in any prose today.

MAXINE. Why, thank you.

BBC INTERVIEWER. You also like to make jokes.

MAXINE. *(Laughs.)* I can't help making jokes. It's a fault, and it gets me in trouble sometimes.

BBC INTERVIEWER. A question about status, or rather the lack of status in being a so-called thriller writer.

MAXINE. The first thing, really, is to define what we're talking about. I mean, if you write novels of suspense like Simenon does and like Eric Ambler does perhaps, in which violence is the background, just as love might be in the background of the ordinary or the straight kind of novel, the mystery story is –

BBC INTERVIEWER. Slightly below the salt?

MAXINE. You can write a long, very lousy historical novel full of sex and it can be a bestseller and be treated respectfully. But a very good thriller writer, who writes far, far better, just gets a little paragraph of course.

BBC INTERVIEWER. Yes, I know. That's very true.

MAXINE. Mostly. There's no attempt to judge the writer as a writer.

BBC INTERVIEWER. But you yourself are judged as a writer, and Dashiell Hammett was, I think –

MAXINE. Well, yes, but how long did it take for that to happen? You starve to death for ten years before your publisher knows you're any good! *(Laughs)*.

BBC INTERVIEWER. *(Laughs.)* Yes, quite!

MAXINE. *(Laughs.)* The publisher, that's what gets a writer thinking about murder!

BBC INTERVIEWER. What sort of murderer would you be?

MAXINE. An overconfident one.

BBC INTERVIEWER. But it takes confidence to pull off a murder, doesn't it?

MAXINE. Yes, but there's confidence and there's cockiness.

BBC INTERVIEWER. So, where do you get your material? Is it always an American setting?

MAXINE. Well, I lived many years in England, but I don't think I could write about it in any sort of realistic way. Of course now, half the writers in America live in England *(Laughs)*.

BBC INTERVIEWER. That's very true.

MAXINE. As far as my material is concerned I'm afraid I get mine by going to places and taking down copious notes because I can't remember anything.

BBC INTERVIEWER. Again to go back to villains.

MAXINE. Of course, the difficulty is to set in oneself and to be able to persuade the reader that your villain not to be pitied for being a sick man. It's difficult to depict somebody who is remorselessly vibrant without being a psychopath. On the other hand, if you create pity for him at once, it's difficult, and that's what I mean about villains. They're very difficult people to build up.

BBC INTERVIEWER. Must he have a very human side?

MAXINE. He may be very kind to his family, but in his business – illegitimate – he may be quite ruthless.

BBC INTERVIEWER. Well, you've got to know these people, you can't invent them. You don't find anyone really that's all bad.

MAXINE. I'm not certain I agree.

BBC INTERVIEWER. We've managed to get an advance copy of your novel, *Your Death Is Necessary*, the one that's just coming out, and I'm very interested in one passage that talks about violence and so on and so forth. It seems to me very well put. Would you be willing to read a bit for us?

MAXINE. I'd love to. To set it up, a man has gone into this girl's bedroom having overheard her conversation as a blackmailer. She brought out a small automatic up from her side. I looked at it.

"Oh guns", I said, "Don't scare me with guns. I've lived with them all my life, I've used an old Derringer, single shots, the kind the riverboat gamblers used to carry. As I got older I graduated to a lightweight sporting rifle then a 303 target rifle and so on. I once made a bull at nine hundred yards at open sight. In case you don't know, the whole target looks the size of a postage stamp at nine hundred yards".

"A fascinating career", she said. "Guns never settle anything", I said. 'They're just a fast curtain to a bad second act'".

BBC INTERVIEWER. *(Chuckles.)* I think that's rather well put.

MAXINE. It's at least a far more sensible point of view than the one which some writers put forward in their books, where people are shooting each other so much and so often that you need a programme to tell who's in the act and who's a spectator.

BBC INTERVIEWER. Do you think there's such a thing as a perfect murder?

MAXINE. Absolutely. On paper, I could plan a murder better than most people, but I doubt I could carry it out.

BBC INTERVIEWER. Really?

MAXINE. Oh, I might be able to carry it out, but in stories things turn out as the author plans them to, in real life they don't. I'd make some stupid mistake and not realize it until the end when I saw that everyone was looking at me.

BBC INTERVIEWER. Yes, yes, quite. Can you give our listeners an example?

MAXINE. Oh, let's see. A housewife makes dinner for her husband. Spaghetti with mushrooms. The husband eats the spaghetti and dies, apparently of a heart attack. As his body is being taken away, something falls from his trouser cuff. They test it. It's full of poison. What fell out of his trouser cuff? A button mushroom.

BBC INTERVIEWER. A button mushroom. Well, now I must remember that the next time my wife offers to make me spaghetti.

MAXINE. Yes, I'd pass on Italian cuisine altogether.

BBC INTERVIEWER. Ha! Very good, very good...

END

www.ingramcontent.com/pod-product-compliance
Lightning Source LLC
Chambersburg PA
CBHW070354120726
47909CB00008B/2841